I0684902

Marcus Bird

BERLIN VANILLA

2

Copyright © 2014 by Marcus Bird

Cover design © 2014 by Marcus Bird

Author photo by Marco Vasquez

ISBN 978-0-9913239-2-0

"We are not the same persons this year as last; nor are those we love. It is a happy chance if we, changing, continue to love a changed person."

- W. Somerset Maugham

BERLIN VANILLA

Chapter One

Kingston is cold.

    It is unseasonal, this weather, which compliments the view before me; the looping arch of a city built near the sea, with the mountains hovering close to the sliding dawn like silent arbiters. There is nothing but the feel of the air on my skin, prickling the membranes and further down into the bones, tingling the tips and the bits. I thought the cold was a long gone thing, something forgotten in the past when I'd lived elsewhere, where Friday nights were blurry memories predicated on the sound of crushed cans under my feet, and the hushed breaths of a girl I might meet late at night. But here I am, standing shirtless on the second floor balcony of my residence, staring out at Kingston's vista. It lies spread-eagled before me, a messy, loosely contiguous set of lights and dark stretches leading everywhere and nowhere. Somewhere, miles away I can see the telltale lights of a police car, flashing indignantly. I can imagine the officer, unsmirking with practiced speech, too ready to harass someone who wasn't lightly complected, checking licenses with eyes doused in compartmentalized bias. This is far from where I am both mentally and physically as my feet stand on cool marble, near a column carved from Lignum Vitae four feet tall. The sculpture is astronomically expensive, but it is a relic from the past, something my parents had bought, parents who are now deep in the ground. The cool tingles my body in a way different from the invasive sense of winter. In a cold climate, the wind, buildings and streets have a blankness to them. The cold touch of architecture seems to compliment the change in the seasons. Brick and sharply contoured sidewalks fit the theme of a chilly night. The cold is abrasive and prickly, like a needle to the fingertips, burning lips and the insides of one's nostrils. This cold here, this Kingston cold, is on the surface. It rolls slowly over my pectorals and my back, traveling slowly up my thighs and near my groin. It is cool enough to make me chilly but not cold, falling into a grey area that reminded my senses of what it had experienced before. Kingston is cold and dark, and tonight I feel as If I am the same way.

But I like it. When I am in the cold I feel more alive and sharper somehow. It makes everything cleaner and clearer, but unfortunately in the night I could only imagine things being different as in front of me the yard and its dark expanse of ghostlike trees offer no touch of man. Behind me, I hear the rustle of bed sheets. There lies Candice, her perfect breasts rising in the darkness like brown mountains. She is on her phone as always, typing to some unknown suitor on her radar. For her, I exist in a periphery of sorts, a person who is neither meaningful nor meaningless. We have known each other since preparatory school, when she was a wild tomboy with a shaggy head of hair, and I was a submissive child who liked to read and paint. When I returned to Kingston some time ago, we drifted into a non-committal relationship that mostly involves raw sexual encounters and me nonchalantly listening to her babble about the social scene. Our connection is as meaningless as the times we meet in my bedroom and her nails scratch my back and her moans beat against the walls. Sometimes in these moments, I think about all those years ago when we met. Back then, our kinship was formed by the water cooler, when she asked me a question I couldn't answer.

"Is the word 'water cooler' an adverb?" she had asked me.

At the time I was remarkably ignorant, and had no answer for her. I tried to chant the inane song we'd practiced in class in my mind, where the little kids would all say:

A verb is an action word!

But sadly, there was no memory trick for an adverb. Was it part adjective and part verb? Or something else? I racked my brain trying to figure out if *water-cooling* was an actual phenomenon, something that the device in front of me was based on. Back then, standing less than five feet tall with dark blue khaki shorts high above my knees, all I knew was pressing the button provided me with liquid refreshment. I also knew that Candice was about five feet three inches tall and intimidating and I didn't want to get a thrashing from her. Yes, she was famous for beating up the boys. Several kids got bloody lips from Candice at the time because of her height advantage and ferocious temper. That day when I stood at the water cooler, fearing retribution from my lack of an answer, she simply eased me aside, but gave me a smile, and pinched me on my shoulder. I have no idea what our connection meant, as we rarely spoke to each other afterward. But years later, in high school, I remembered seeing her again. Then I was somewhat taller and becoming a man, with my shoulders fanning out and a touch more muscle on my body. I'd lost some of the boyish shyness and developed the dull bravado of a young man with no fear of the future. Candice had maintained the same height, but her body had begun to change. The angry, flat-chested tomboy was now a sculpture in formation. The slight swell of her breasts showed under her school dress, and her face was a thing of beauty. High school is dull to some extent now, but I always remember when she came up to me and pinched me on the shoulder, mentioning something about the water cooler and then running to her friends and giggling. My days were filled with fantasizing about playing football in the evenings and dreading class. I'd run in the sun until my skin was shiny and black, and often I'd get cursed by my father for not being in front of the school at three-thirty when he'd arrive to pick me up. High school, such a time of limited expectations.

But now I'm standing on a balcony as a man, and Kingston is cold. Candice is behind me, naked and unaware of my ponderings, lost in her digital world. Like most people Candice has no idea that I want to die. This feeling isn't something I can easily explain. My parents died when I was a teenager, and many people ask me if this adversely affected me. I cannot truly remember if it did. I love my parents, but the day they met in an accident and were gone, I don't exactly remember how I felt. A counselor I saw sometime afterward mentioned to me that I was suppressing images and memories but I didn't agree with him. Many years have passed since the day I received the news, and I have never shed a tear.

Like many Jamaicans, I decided to go abroad to university. It was in a small town somewhere in Pennsylvania, where my Jamaican-ness was heralded as something great. That was where I first experienced the bitter cold of winter, but there were often young women to share my bed, stealing away the unrepentant sensation of outside in heated exchanges of bodily fluids. Nothing was bad. I liked my classes, some professors and I even joined the college soccer team. But one day, a year or so before my parents died, on an afternoon like any other, I left the cafeteria and went into my room. I slipped *My Own Prison,* Creed's first album into my CD player and turned it up. That was my first Americana album, filled with heavy rock riffs and pop ballads. But then, I felt a crushing sensation of darkness overwhelm me. My vision became blurry and I felt low and quiet. Things seemed to slow, and I could feel a tightness in my fingertips. Like water leaking from a bucket, my resolve drained quickly. Soon I had no mood, and the music blasting from my CD player had no effect on me. I turned it off, trapped in the despair of the moment, frightened by what I was feeling. Nothing was relevant. The wooden construction of my dorm bed, the posters of random Rock bands on the wall, a t-shirt some girl left under my bed. Meaning evaporated.

There was nothing else that remained in the elements of the day that held anything familiar. The touch of water on my face in the morning had lost its merit, the sensation of cool sheets slipping off my body in the morning signaling a step into the day was a beggar's palm devoid of alms. Sounds and images became a trickle. If a day was an assortment of fluctuations, events and patterns, it was more like an LP set on 'slow' with some reggae idol talking in a hauntingly deep voice. The absence of something challenges the need for it, but who thinks about the absence of a desire to live? It is akin to an absence of a desire to breathe. Breathing simply is, like the sweat-laced brow of a farmer on a hot day, or black soot after a fire has died. The vacuum had arrived, and it was incomprehensible and subsequently horrifying. As time has passed I've learned to adjust to aspect of life being a dull hum. Generally I'm sitting beside a washing machine permanently on the spin cycle, the inner gears of the machine providing that *shhhhmmmmm* that makes people introspect when doing laundry. It is an overarching tone that is the metronome for everything around me, only broken by a handful of things. Sexual encounters are one thing that help, but a belief in the pointlessness of life extends to a sense of pointlessness in many things. Women come and go, dissipating like ectoplasmic beings. Some tickle my fancy, pulling me out of the dark deluge for a moment, the sighs and moans and our mutual slick favoring a possible escape from the blank, but after she is gone it returns, and I'm lying naked somewhere staring at nothing, listening to my heartbeat. *Nihilism,* a counselor had said to me, was possibly what was happening, though she couldn't figure out what a trigger might be to pull me out of the muck.

My phone rings, and I answer it.

"Yo boss you coming through later?" a voice says to me.

I murmur a reply, then hang up.

Some people call me a promoter, others a party boy. I'm somewhere in the middle. For a year or two I threw a small event at a friend's house called *Inside.* The party was garbage. We had a few cheap plastic tables with bottles of rum from his dad's basement, bleary-eyed neighbourhood teens trying to act older sneaking in, and us hanging about, ten to twenty of us initially drinking, smoking and popping pills. Soon the word spread about this free party with free drinks and it grew from twenty people to one hundred in six months. Between my friend and myself, we'd always get high fives and pats on the back from dudes I didn't recognize with red eyes. It was also a time of ridiculous sexual exploration. Any young man who throws a popular party in Kingston has godlike power. The ability to get a girl into a place free or provide her drinks is a most powerful aphrodisiac. We made names for ourselves because of our escapades. My good friend and partner in promoting the party, Andrew, I briefly called *Gyalvester Stallone,* after Sylvester Stallone, and he called me *Gyallison Ford,* after Harrison Ford. Some bright spark at one party told everyone to call me Indiana Jones and for some reason the name stuck. To most people, I am Indie. After a fight broke out and some idiot businessman pulled a gun on his friend, the party was over. But I cashed in on that that credibility for some time. Guys better than me at doing parties and promotions invited me to their events. I got tickets for stage shows, girls who remembered wild nights at *Inside* still texted me at all hours of the morning. This time of life I could say was somewhat enjoyable. That sense of the night air on my skin, the smell of rum and cigarette smoke in the air blanketed by raucous voices.

****

I go inside the parking lot and immediately hear an old Beres Hammond track blasting from the dark insides of a silver Honda Civic, the driver a steely-eyed guy with a shovel jaw and blood red eyes. Some guy is pissing behind a Range Rover exactly like mine, but it is Cobalt blue. The Honda Civic dude races through the parking lot, rubber squelching as he rips into a space beside the SUV, causing the man taking the piss to be momentarily exposed by his high beams. Two girls with long blonde wigs walk past with somnambulant gaits, warped by the undulating asphalt. Three short, light-skinned fellows walk by wearing matching outfits of worn out Polos and baggy jeans. One is laughing excitedly and I can see the animation in his face is an illusion because his eyes dart too quickly left to right. His friends nod with a similar, odd energy and they coast in their cloud of social awkwardness past the vehicle. I don't need to move yet. My Comme Des Garcons shirt feels nice against my skin, but better against the leather car seat. The windshield is my window to this ambulant theater of people entering a lame party. The tint is heavy, and it would be hard for anyone to see me without squinting, but to me, they are plain as day. Men with dirty NY caps and fake Chuck Taylors, ambiguously gay dancer types with oppressively tight pants and the occasional skin bleached face. Girls with wigs that look like a taxidermied cat, industry types who dress uber-plain but walk with more confidence than a guy nearby them in a silver jacket, and a few wanna be it girls, walking forward a few steps then stopping to check her phone for a message that will never arrive. I like the menagerie of oddity. It is amusing because I cannot amuse myself. There is no way to predict who I will see in this parking lot. Shaggy could stroll in with an entourage; even Neyo might pop by in shorts and his trademark fedora. But mostly it is a stream of the usual folks, people escaping the day by diving into the shadows at night. I like my pants more than my shirt. It is a polyester blend that stays cool long after I've shut off the car's air conditioning. Shirts and pants of this quality make me feel like an extension of the car; invisibly perched in a ground level tower. Soon, I grow tired of people watching and come out of the car. A few people see me exit the vehicle and flinch briefly despite themselves. I know these looks and body ticks. A young man with a car like this shouldn't exist in this economy. He shouldn't exist in the world. My face is flat as I walk forward and the sharp pinch of that Kingston cold touches my nose. It makes me feel calm knowing that my pants will stay cool longer. I bump fists with the security guard and the guy selling soup from a large pot near the entrance. Two people tap me immediately, a banker recently returned to Jamaica I met after a bender at some new bar off Hope Road, and a guy I see around whose name I can't remember that always pronounces my full name when greeting me. A girl I slept with a year before shoots me an icy look, and I get a nod from a guy who throws a major party in the country twice a year. Three more steps and I'm slapped on the arm by a guy who met his long term girlfriend at *Inside,* and then I see two high school friends at a table already well into their second bottle of white rum. By the DJ are the usual suspects; industry people of varying levels of interest. Some hot girls with jaded eyes, other DJs with the casual energy of men who don't need to hunt for pussy, guys hanging around to be seen with these people and then people who don't know anyone there who are just standing by. The DJ calls my name on the microphone and I nod at him, high fiving an artiste who wants me to manage him but I always tell him I don't have time. Another girl I slept with, this one who wants me comes over and says an awkward hello and I go to the bar when *Old Dog Like Me* starts playing over the airwaves. I order a bottle of Appleton and they take it to a table I usually have, but some people are sitting there so I go over to the DJ section and rest it near a wall. Three people ask me for drinks and I wave at the bottle. A girl touches my shirt and tells me she likes it. I ask her to figure out the brand. She tugs the back a little too hard to see the tag and I feel the fabric almost tear. Annoyed, I walk away, leaving the liquor on the table and stand with two guys that rap, smoking blunts by a wall tinged in smoke.

I chat with them for a little while, feeding off their positive energy. It is an energy from the raw well of their unbridled passion; and I sink my fangs into it. I walk back to the table and fix myself a drink. A heavy hand lands on my shoulder and I see a vaguely familiar face looking back at me, a young man in his early twenties with the faded features of someone who drinks and smokes too much. "Indiana Jones" he says with a smile. I greet him heartily and offer him a drink. We talk about an upcoming party, "Twilight" that will be held at Hope Gardens and he salutes me as he walks away with his drink and proceeds to dance with a fat girl in bright yellow spandex. I make another drink, noting to myself I have no idea who that fellow is. More people come around the table, including the silly girl from earlier who almost tore my shirt. I take my bottle and go to the other side of the venue, resting it near a table shrouded by guys with thick locks in bright Tams with blood-shot eyes. I'm back in the car again in my mind; watching the people move to and fro in a blur, the liquor is now making things slower and dull. The music is picking up and I'm not really feeling anything much, except the taste of Pepsi and Appleton on my lips, sweetened by nearby plumes of cigarette smoke. I say hello to more people, my smile practiced and responses witty and glib-soaked. The faces are all fragments merging into a shapeless form in the city. This routine repeats until the bottle is half empty, and my bladder is bursting at the seams. I stroll towards the bathroom, not before seeing Andrew. We shake hands and exchange genuine smiles. I point him to where my bottle is and lumber to the bathroom. Inside, a fellow takes unusual interest in my clothing and keeps speaking to me as he pisses beside me at the opposite urinal.

"I'm not a faggot," I mumble.

The man, with his hair covered in extensions made to look like braids freezes, his face an indignant mask, but I am already outside, while he is still relieving himself. A girl exiting the women's bathroom gives me a quick eye, but her body is swamped in a splotchy mess of bad tattoo work. An off duty bartender I know hits my shoulder and tells me to come by for a free drink the next day. I nod and go back to Andrew who is chatting to me about two girls standing near where my bottle was.

"I heard about this place but it looks rough."

"Yeah tonight is a little bit on the sausage fest side."

"It's a damn *Man Army* in here," Andrew says.

"Very *manful,*" I reply.

Swigging his drink, Andrew says, "No, it's a *manimal farm.*"

I raised my arms over my head and started gesturing.

"It's a manhouse, a MANHOUUSSE!"

We both laugh heartily.

More liquor flows and the evening starts to dissipate like the swirls of smoke drifting into oblivion above us. After the bottle is finished we head up to Hope Gardens. Briefly there has been a Friday event happening there. Andrew drives a black Honda Civic, which flies up Hope Road in a roar of smoke and rubber. I trail behind in no rush listening to some show on the radio talking about sex.

"So my boyfriend always wants anal sex, but I am not into that, what should I do?" comes a concerned female voice.

The host responds with some politically correct textbook answer and I switch to Irie FM and hear Ken Boothe's "Train is Coming" echo through the speakers. Even though outside is chilly I have the air conditioning on full blast. It is keeping me sharp. My phone is vibrating, and I assume Andrew is already at Hope Gardens. When I pull in there are cars everywhere and the bipedal remnants of the fading night dribbling into the shadows. I nod at the security and walk in with Andrew. There is some kind of list, but lists rarely matter these days. We head to the bar and get anther bottle of Appleton, and go to a table near the dance floor.

"This place is always so pale," Andrew says.

"Pale like you."

"Don't knock my skin colour man, I'm a Paleontologist."

Andrew is shorter than me with skin the colour of sand. Some people occasionally say hello to Andrew, mostly white Jamaicans who give me a perfunctory nod as they engage him in conversation. I'm not taking anything in, instead I watch the wind sway the tall leaves of some trees in the distance, wondering what is hidden within the darkness of the park, if something is out there watching me as I am watching it. The fresh bottle of rum looms before me, waiting to be defiled. I make a drink and go through the crowd leaving Andrew talking with his friends. I say hello to a few Embassy guys I partied with the week before at a mixer at Terra Nova and hug a girl I know who is some kind of big designer but I've never been to any of her fashion shows. Someone taps me and I turn around but it seems they thought I was someone else and kept walking. A tall blonde girl with sharp features whispers "Comme Des Garcons, nice pick" into my ear but is gone before I can say anything else to her. I go to the portable bathroom and chat briefly with a woman handing out paper towels, then relieve myself in some nearby bushes. Washing my hands by the portable bathroom, a guy hails me. He is of average height with an indiscernible ethnicity. There are about twenty of his doppelgangers in the party.

"Indie! What's up bro?"

I pause for a moment, wondering to myself which genius decided to import the word *bro* and make it a fashionable world in the uptown parlance.

"Nothing much *bro*," I reply.

"You going to Twilight?" the guy says.

"I dunno man, how what's the damage?"

"The party is like six grand bro."

"Too bad I sold my other kidney last week," I say.

The guy laughs in a giggle and asks me why he doesn't have my number, but I tell him I have his and go back into the party. On the dance floor I see Candice, her eyes briefly lock with mine, but she says nothing. In an exquisite silver dress with matching heels, she's standing head and shoulders over a short bald man wearing a black polo shirt making drinks at a table. I drift away and even though I have a bottle I go to the bar and order a gin and tonic and sip it. Nearby me, I see some possible candidates. Technically you could say these women were beautiful, but their faces were hard, masked in the unrepentant backwash of being burned over and over. They stand, waiting to be saved; with their long fake hair, long fake nails and long fake stares. They are doing their best to project casual discomfort. Their backs are high and arched, the lights around bouncing a little too brightly off the false hair, the makeup a little too thick and clay-like. Out of courtesy I say hello. I challenge a girl to do a shot with me and she shuffles awkwardly, flashes her eyelashes and says some non-committal statement. I'm already bored. She isn't very cute.

"What's your name," I say to her friend.

"Why would you ask that?" she replies.

"Why would I ask you your name?"

"Yes, I can't see why you'd ask that."

I take my shot, give the girls a faux Japanese bow and head back to the dance floor. Statues like them are everywhere; standing in the shadows with drinks in hand, ice cubes clinking in unison with the throbbing of bass beats. I go back to the table where Andrew is entertaining two short girls with long curly hair. I fix a drink and nod at one of the girls, who doesn't say hello. Andrew is smiling and looking deeply into the eyes of one girl, who is laughing at everything he is saying.

"Looks like you guys should go take a ride in your *Wonder Civic*," I say to Andrew.

"No man, I think her friend wouldn't mind a drive in your *Strange Rover*," Andrew replies.

The girl turns to me.

"You drive a Range Rover?"

We have more drinks and suddenly the night is cheery again. The bottle of rum is half done and the girls are drinking it with no reservation. One is Britney and the other is Brittany. I keep mixing up their names, but whomever I'm talking to doesn't seem to care. She's standing very close now, her eyes glazed with liquor.

"We want to go to Twilight," she says, gesturing at her friend.

"I see."

She slips a thin hand around my waist. "You and Andrew should take us."

"Definitely," I reply.

I don't remember the rest of the conversation because I'm on auto-pilot. I stare into her eyes and into the scenery around me searching for something amidst the chaos. I look at the statues of the women waiting to be saved, as the music coasts over our heads. Brittany or Britney intermittently checks her phone while we are talking, smiling and giggling as she makes more drinks with the rum on the table. A young man in a faded Polo shirt comes over and slaps Andrew on the shoulder.

"Andrew the fucking ladies man, how are you sir?"

"I'm good *bro,*" Andrew responds.

"We are heading down to Sixty-Nine, you and Britney should come through."

"Yes we should," Britney chimes in.

Behind Andrew stands a girl on the edge of reason, wobbly and trying to maintain her composure, sending me fractured smiles through a constant squinting of her eyes. There is beauty in there somewhere, albeit fading slowly. Her hair is long and luxuriant, and the firm outline of a well-maintained body shows through the open blazer she wears with a Bandeau top underneath. I imagine her years before, blazing a trail on the Kingston circuit, being wined and dined by quality men, now living a life relegated to subpar guys and late night trips to dirty strip clubs.

I ignore Brittany and go to her.

"Are you a sixty nine kind of girl?"

The woman smiles at me, forgetting herself and rears up to maintain proper composure.

"Depends on what kind you are talking about," she replies.

I give her a crocodile smile and go back to the table and make another drink. I hand this to her.

"Oh I don't need any more Bryan made sure I'm super drunk, I think he wants to take advantage of me," she whispers in a smoky voice, gesturing at him with the crook of her nose.

She takes the drink from me anyway and gulps it greedily, her eyes more sultry and intoxicating. Bryan raises his eyebrows into a smile and steps towards me with his hand extended.

"This girl is a riot. What's your name bro?"

"Indie," I reply.

"You should come through too Indie, some of my friends have a booth there already, high roller type deal."

"Sounds good," I say.

The chaos around me is slowly forming into something interesting. The tapestry of the night is providing its usual mix of intrigue. My phone buzzes in my pants and I see a text from Candice:

Where R U?

Brittany's eyes grow wide and she grabs my phone.

"Wow you have the new iPhone! I really want to get this model."

It is beholden to her, this device, with its illusory gold carapace. Status screams from its tiny speakers, diving into the canals of her ear, saying things words never could. I take the phone from her.

"Careful, you might see all my sex videos and what not."

"Dirty boy are we?"

"Nothing wrong with a little camera fun," I say to her.

Andrew laughs at our dialogue and says we should head out. Brittany is coming with me. Like the bipedal remnants floating around before, we join the shadowy fray, traipsing with uneven footfalls on dirt and grass towards my car. With a hiss, the hydraulics raise the car up and it is at the ready, black and obvious like the night. Brittany's body language is something else now, and she happily curls up in the front seat without her seatbelt on. She fiddles with the radio and puts it on Zip 103 FM.

"I hate this station," I say.

"How can you hate Zip? Everyone loves it," she says, running her hand along the wood on the dashboard.

"They play the same songs day in day out, don't you get bored with a lack of creativity?"

"I like pop songs," she replies.

"Pop songs are like spurious gemstones," I say.

"What's spurious?" she asks.

"Who's curious?" I reply.

She laughs as I pull out my camera and take a picture of her, smiling. She doesn't realize how high her skirt is hiked up above her knees, or maybe she does.

"Safety first," I say pointing to her seatbelt as the car comes on in a roar.

She giggles again and takes the Appleton bottle out of the car's cooler, fixing a drink. Again I'm on Hope Road, but this time Sean Paul's "She Doesn't Mind" is playing over the airwaves. Brittany sings along with the song, tells me about a friend she think hooked up with Sean Paul or some guy who looked exactly like him, then notices that we are driving through a consistent stream of green lights. In front of us, a barrage of flashing blue lights makes me nervous. A white minivan is on its side in a pool of shattered glass. The police have no interest in me as the car rolls by.

"How the hell did that happen?" Brittany says.

"I have no idea," I say, turning onto Lady Musgrave road. The song is still playing after the lights fade behind us and we pull in front of Sixty-Nine. Three men wearing safety vests rush to the car immediately, gesturing and working hard to help me park, even though I already am. I don't wind down the windows and sit with Brittany for a while, and fix another drink. I see Andrew's car parked nearby. A man is still by the window, his voice muted as he tries to say something to me. I know he cannot see me through the heavy tint of the windows, and eventually, he walks away. Then I see Andrew somewhere in the parking lot, with Bryan and the girl wearing the blazer. We head out and join them and are ushered into the club. In the darkness I see a dancehall artiste or two sipping champagne and looking bored, two of the people I'd seen at the event earlier, including the guy who had spoken to me that I didn't know. He is there with the same fat girl her yellow spandex pants, sitting near the catwalk where a tall woman with very dark skin deals with the pole expertly. We pass the catwalk and head towards the booth, which is cordoned off the main area up a flight of stairs. The bouncer nods at me (he used to work at a club I once frequented) and I join a throng of people sitting on a huge plush couch for V.I.Ps. Everyone looks like Bryan, pale and of mixed ethnicity. One or two guys I recognize vaguely from outings on the road, but I know no one else. Andrew gives one of the guys a hearty hello and Bryan introduces me to the group.

"Guys this is Indie," he says.

"Indie!" they chant in unison.

A shot of Patrón is thrust into my hand and I pass it to Brittany, who smells it before swallowing it. The girl in the blazer is watching me, her eyes wet with alcohol, her legs lightly apart. I walk to the bathroom and take a piss, hearing the unusual buzz of the door vibrating from the sound of the club's speakers. I muse on the idea of internal acoustics. Most strip clubs would eventually deafen its workers, I surmise. Staying in there day in and day out in a place that's too loud and too wild. Someone comes into the bathroom. It's the girl in the blazer.

"I want to suck you off," she says.

I am shocked by this bluntness. Such bluntness is not common nor expected. Her eyes are demanding resolution, her lips parted and ready. I pause for a moment, and I see her pupils are dilated.

"Give me some of the good stuff first," I say, rubbing her on the cheek.

She smiles and tugs a vial from her pants, wiggling it in front of me. I dab a bit of the powder on my finger and inhale quickly, giving her a kiss on the cheek.

"People will see us, but I'll take your number," I say.

She growls and licks my neck in a strange way and with lightning dexterity punches her number into my phone. Her name is Selena.

"I have the same phone," she purrs.

"A woman of taste I see."

"Many tastes," she says with a delectable smile.

I leave her in the bathroom and head to Brittany, who is watching Andrew get a lap dance from Britney. A stripper joins the fray, and the guys in the group pull out thick wads of thousand dollar bills, tossing them at her while pouring rum on her breasts. The stripper gestures to a nipple, and one of the guys hungrily licks it while his friend pours rum on his lips. The group cheers.

"Isn't it interesting how strip clubs are this after party spot now? I mean like ten years ago people just went home at two a.m. Now it's 'Let's go to Sixty-Nine' or whichever club happens to be open. But you know what, they should take a page from the club in the states. See in the states a lot of strip clubs have buffets, because *ahem* after people have imbibed a significant amount of the good stuff naturally they want to ease it down with a snack, so instead of going to Burger King or some late night eatery, they get their entertainment and food at the same time. Yeah? Does that make sense to you madame?"

"I guess so," Brittany says, rubbing my thigh. "But I wouldn't feel safe eating food at a strip club."

"Well it would just be about licensing. Getting a food permit isn't that hard as long as regulations are watched and spot checks show that the food is being prepared in a manner that is hitherto considered appropriate and adequate relative to the needs of the patronage for that establishment. Effectively, a strip club can be both a restaurant and a den of debauchery. Entrepreneurially speaking being a restaurateur is simply a matter of space, time and market. Once the overheads are factored in one just needs marketing and the spread of user interest along the lines of public relations and simple strategies for campaigns. Seeing how Strip clubs are now the *de facto* after party activity, it is just a matter of the management and their philosophy on how well they create that comingling of what some may call culinary cunnilingus."

"Culinary cunnilingus! You are funny," she says to me leaning closer.

"And you are sexy," I reply.

We forget about the party and the backseat of the car is now the world. She masterfully pulls my throbbing bulge from my pants and takes me in her mouth. The world is crystal clear as little beads of sweat dot my forehead. She wants me to go down on her but I don't, instead I play with her breasts and the nape of her neck. The air conditioning is on full blast and the world outside is oblivious to our carnal frolicking. Her body is dark and scattered with tan lines. She is unusually wet and ready for me. I thrust into the darkness with her legs around my back emboldened and powered by my little white friend, spinning and turning through the highways of my bloodstream. She moans but I can't hear her, in the horizon of my mind is an inkling of a feeling. It is not the feeling of her between my legs, it isn't the touch of her nipples against my Comme Des Garcons shirt, it is the tiniest iota of a good feeling. I thrust faster as my arms reach for it in my mind; it dances and flutters around, elusive and giggling. Brittany comes hard and clutches me as I keep going, my teeth gritted because I'm searching for that light again, but it is gone, lost in the darkness, hidden in the tint of an invisible world. I come as well, shaking and shuddering in the arms of this girl I've known for two hours. I hold her for a moment, and it almost feels genuine, then Sean Paul's "She Doesn't Mind" starts playing again and I laugh, a real and genuine laugh.

Then Brittany asks me about my phone again, wondering why I have two of the same model. She purrs and asks me to give her one, but I say no and she gets indignant and leaves the vehicle going back inside the club. I drive home slowly, savouring the cool breeze touching my face. Then back at my house, the vast empty space of the mansion greets me without applause. The night fades rapidly into the past, dragged away without fanfare by mystical harpies. I go inside and walk through the darkness back onto the balcony and stare out at Kingston, rubbing my arms because of the cold.

Chapter Two

There is nothing more tragic than an unusually expensive dinner. I think about this while picking at my food and looking at a godawful Faberge Egg in the middle of the table that has no commonality with the tartan cloth it rests on. Add to that the nature of my plate, which is blue. Such plates psychologically make people eat less, which is counterintuitive in restaurant culture, but I'm the only person on the sidelines that cares apparently. The meal is typical of its ilk, nonexistent bordering on unfilling, extravagantly described in print but underwhelming in reality. I'm tempted to become one of those breatharians, subsisting on light and air but my stomach growls in protest. I'm sitting with Ed, the fabulously wealthy spawn of one of Jamaica's richest business dynasties who I went to high school with. He spits out a grape seed to the floor, remarking about the nature of presentation and the ideas behind seedless grapes.

"What about authenticity?" I argue.

"Authenticity is a product of the environment not what sits on my plate in front of me," he replies.

"How so?"

"Authentic cuisine is essentially a misnomer. Nothing cooked in a kitchen and brought out to you can be authentic anymore. Real creation happens within the place of origin of said dish."

"So if I go to St. Mary and feast on a freshly fatted goat I'm having authentic cuisine?"

"Most certainly."

"What then, if said fatted goat was quickly transported to Kingston and then served to me in short order, wouldn't it be authentic?"

"Transportation is filled with contaminants. The goat would need to be preserved, thus removing the immediacy of its authenticity."

"But *some* authenticity is worth it no? Better to have a goat doused in some Benzyl-alkaline whatever solution than eat it as is and get the runs for days."

"My point is proven."

"How then does this relate to grapes?"

"Obviously the chef want us to *feel* like we were having an authentic Italian meal, so he put grapes with actual seeds in it."

"Who says people in Italy like seeds in their grapes?"

"That's not the point. If I'm in Italy, I'm having authentic cuisine."

"Authenticity is relative to ingredients and chef skill."

Ed laughs. "God made food; the devil the cooks.'

"Throwing James Joyce at me won't make your point any more meaningful. I think you are talking about the pretentious nature of someone that *believes* they are giving you something authentic."

"Of course. A man who can cook Jerk chicken can cook it anywhere but to tell me a meal is authentic or not is relative to whether I have experienced it before and the extent to which I have knowledge of what I am eating."

"How pretentious," I say.

"This cook is pretentious. Giving me damn seeded grapes to make a point. The nerve."

"Indeed, the nerve."

After the meal we leave and head to The Cube, a new art space in the middle of New Kingston. It is exactly like its namesake, a long stretch of space with few frills along the walls. A hotshot designer named Connie is throwing a fashion show there, which means lots of interesting people and free booze.

"This place should technically be called *Cuboid,*" Ed says.

"People say the Earth is a sphere but its geoid," I reply.

"Exactly," Ed says with a laugh.

There are seats arranged near a simple but elegant runway, but few people are sitting down. Bodies hug the borders of the establishment, clinging to the shadows. The first person I see is Usain Bolt, taking a picture with a short young woman, squealing with delight and she gestures to her friend taking the photo with her cell phone.

"*La Petite Mort* is here," I mumble to Ed.

"The little death? Are you calling him a euphemism?"

"A legendary euphemism of course," I reply with a smile.

"A girl I know called him a walking orgasm," Ed says.

I chuckle, and take a glass of red wine from a waiter.

"Interesting how the world loves you when you are famous. Guys like us have to deal with the frosty types unused to a life around the darker complected folk."

Ed takes a glass of wine from another waiter, and gives Sean Paul a hearty handshake.

"You are wrong Ed," I say, "You are Ed Walker, you aren't black."

"What? I'm darker than you," Ed says, swigging his wine.

"Yes, but your family owns half of Jamaica. Didn't your father just open a new bank?"

"People need places to put their money," Ed says with a smile. "So I'm not black because of who I am?"

"Yes, you've squired enough of the hottest girls for me to know that prejudice does not follow a man wearing Russell and Bromley shoes."

"Ha! You saw that! Good eye! So I guess this relates to what you said about Bolt?'"

"Of course, Bolt isn't black either, he is simply Bolt."

"You mean in the way that Brad Pitt isn't white, he is Brad Pitt?"

"Exactly. Very few people have the chance to step beyond the paradigms of their pathetic lives."

"Pathetic? My life isn't pathetic."

"It has to be. Have you completely explored your potential in all directions? Sexually, physically, monetarily, statusarily?"

"Statusarily isn't a word," he replies.

"I'm *making it* a word," I say, grabbing another glass of wine from a passing waiter. "Our lives are wasted little bottles of potential we've never fully opened. It trickles out like piss from an old man's bladder."

I take a deep drink of the wine, and nod at Christopher Martin and his manger.

"In the land of the blind, the one-eyed God is king," Ed mutters while smiling at a short girl with a giant but perfect derriere.

"Are you calling me myopic Mr. Ed?"

"Are you calling me a horse Mr. Indie?"

The allusion is lost on me until I remember the TV show with the talking horse and I laugh weakly.

"I am not myopic. I am simply stating the reality of a pervasive situation. There are individuals who will be the ultimate versions of themselves, while we just sit here and drink and chase around each other trying our best to get laid."

We get pulled into a group that knows Ed, and I see a familiar face from the night before. He is short and broad-shouldered with a dark brown complexion. In another life I could see him as a man who would be lifting things and leading men. Perhaps he would be a blacksmith, standing by a roaring fire, face speckled with moisture as the hammer sends its tinny wail into the black bosom of nearby smoke. In a tight, shiny black jacket and fitted Levis he is poorly squeezing this workman image into the narrow folds of hipsterdom. He is also the man who was lasciviously enjoying the stripper's nipples the night before. His name is Gregory and he is some bank executive. In the group is Taurus Riley and a hotshot editor from the Jamaica Observer, a producer who apparently just did Beenie Man's latest hit track, and a few aging models who don't bother to identify what agency they are from. Ed starts his usual game of chatting about nothing in particular and I leave the group and walk up to Connie, who is standing by a table.

"I'll need three shirts right now," I say, giving her a hug.

"Three? With only one design?" she replies.

She is on her phone looking at something important, but her body language tells me I have her complete attention.

"Now Connie, where is your business acumen, I could be offering a boon to your launch, behaving extravagantly or simply just buying three because I want three."

"True. What do you think of the launch setup?" she asks, her eyes still focused on her cellphone.

"Everyone is here, that is all that matters."

"When Bolt walked in I was pretty shocked."

"You know what shocked me?"

"What?"

"That fellow in the gabardine. What a tragedy."

Connie laughs loudly and a few people nearby turn and smile at us, their eyes dripping with boredom and pregnant with the wish for a conversation like ours.

"You are funny," Connie says.

Proteje's manager comes over and says something to her, and I leave them and walk between Bounty Killer and a few rough looking members of his entourage, go towards the side doors where I see a few execs from one of the big phone companies have setup camp. I say hello to another embassy person and a person touches me, another fellow from the strip club night, then I eat a few tasty gourmet eggs from the table nearest to the DJ and sip on another glass of wine. Everyone is clamouring around everyone, all smiles, hugs and hearty hellos. I feel slightly sorry for a fellow who wore a dark green suit to this occasion, but he is accompanied by an outstanding girl who I can see is fresh to this world. Her eyes dart around as she sees all the celebrities, many of whom no doubt see her and need a new flavor of the week. Sharks get excited when blood is in the water, and soon I see a wealthy businessman approach her, his body language perfect and practiced. He says something to the young man, immediately disarming him, and then a minute later the girl is laughing and drinking from his table while the kid in the green suit stares into his phone, waiting for messages that will never arrive. There is a flurry of attention at the door as Junior Gong and some of the Marleys walk in briskly and head towards and empty corner of the lobby. The DJ immediately calls his name on the microphone, and plays "Welcome to Jamrock". Connie motions for me to sit in the second row of seats near the runway, and I sit beside in between Alaine and some guy who had a hit song years ago that I can't remember the name of. I see Neyo near the front row, talking to Shaggy. I excuse myself to go to the bathroom and I wonder to myself how the hell Connie knows all these people. A hand pinches me and I see Candice, wearing a form fitting black skirt. She is effortlessly attractive and I feel my loins tingle with familiarity. She is with another man this time, equally short as the last one. He gives me a nod and a smirk, no doubt reveling in memories of the night before.

"Hey," she says to me.

"Sorry, I don't talk to criminals," I reply.

Her face floods with surprise.

"Because you are criminally hot," I muse.

The anguished look dissipates oddly into one with a smile, and she pinches me again. She says nothing, just looking at me, and I hop from one foot to another.

"The bathroom beckons," I say to her.

She turns away from me, hugging a tall middle-eastern looking fellow giving her a sleazy eye and I drift to the bathroom. The guy wearing the gabardine and the dark glasses seems to be rotating to any position where a high number of people would walk past him. Earlier he was posted by the doorway, with his hands in his pockets, his dark glasses covered eyes unreadable. Then he was by the bar, waving 'no' to waiters offering him drinks. Now he was near the bathroom, hands in his pockets again. A photographer motioned for him to take a picture and he was quickly at the ready, posing and pointing a finger forward. In the bathroom, I see Tristan, a young doctor I know. I take the opposite urinal.

"I say doc, can I can any diseases from urinal splash back?"

He laughs and tells me it is highly unlikely, and asks me if I'm good. I say no, and he nods. After we wash our hands we go outside. I follow him through a sea of SUVs to his Audi Q8. He opens the backdoor and zips open a black bag filled with bottles. I get three bottles of Adderal, two Ambien and a Xanax.

"Any codeine?" I ask.

"Not right now," he replies with a smile, counting my money in his hands.

"Who bought it the rest of it?"

"You wouldn't believe me if I told you," he replies.

"The many layers of Kingston's gilded cage," I say, walking away.

I tuck the bottles into my satchel and go back into the event space. I see supermodel Janelle Mckenzie sipping on a glass of wine chatting to a theatre actor. One of the guys from the No-Maddz rolls in, in tight black pants and a silver vest. I look for my seat but an old white guy is sitting there talking to a girl who I realize is Brittany. In her hand is a brand new gold iPhone. Turning around I almost collide with a sea of pale Jamaicans chatting loudly in highly inflected voices. I see Ed by one of the bars in heavy conversation with the girl with the huge ass we'd seen earlier, and I go to the opposite one, nodding at Selena, the girl I'd met the night before who doesn't flinch or look at me. I get a Vodka and ginger ale and drink it quickly standing by a wall. I close my eyes for a moment as the DJ says the fashion show is about to start and I feel another hand touch me and I see Amy standing in front of me. Amy, the first girl I ever loved.

No one can be the world, but she was in those days with overcast skies and the rumbling of the city somewhere in the distance, where all exploration took place for the first time. Our bodies and minds were adorned with fresh boots to take murky steps into the world of adulthood. I was fascinated by her profile, the short interesting nose, full thick lips and a face halfway between round and square. She was the first girl to kiss me and slip her hands down my pants, the little fingers probing through the pubic hair. She was identity and reason.

It wasn't just he thrill of seeing her naked, it was the expectancy that was the most powerful. Wanting to see her day after day, wanting to hear her laugh or complain about something. Smelling her light scent of sweat if she'd been exercising, or feeling the tingle of her fingers on my thighs as we watched a movie. It was a time when there was still some sensation to things, separate from the dull hum of whatever existence was now. There was a time a young man offended her, and my anger was pure. She had been besmirched, the girl the held my heart, the girl whose body my lips had traveled and whose mind my legs had galloped through. It took twenty minutes of coaxing and cajoling for her to calm me down, and later our passion was at its highest fever pitch. I wanted all of her at once, her mind, her skin, her life intertwined with mine. I saw glimpses of the future, glimpses of things that could be. Then there was a shift. Some other guy emerged from the Kingston swamp and swept her out of my arms and far away. He took her mind and her body. Later I saw the signs too easily. The time I had called her.

"Hey baby," I had said.

"Sorry I can't talk to you now, I'm walking with someone," she had replied.

"No problem," I had said with a smile, thinking of her hours before, slipping off her boy shorts and standing in front of me with the body only an eighteen year old could have. I didn't think the idea of *someone* was anything at all, that it was a person other than me, because in the world it was her and me. But I was wrong of course, and as she started slipping away, I knew what the word *someone* really meant. Doubt plagued me and thoughts I'd never had swarmed about my mind in an eerie pattern choppy and disorganized like a Charlie Chaplin film. I choked on the idea of her with someone else. I felt broken by the reality of something I couldn't control. The excitement I felt looking forward to seeing her each day became an acute form of dread, the dull hum was set on low. Was he white? Was he black, was he in between? Was he rich? What about him did she like? Did he have a huge schlong? Memories became malevolent wardens, teasing me with images from the past as I fell into the cold casket of permanent realization. I masturbated thinking of her, crying afterwards. Anger constantly raged through my system as I fought to forget her. My father told me that most women were bitches and I needed to get some new pussy to forget about her. He loaned me his Benz a few times when I was going out but nothing happened. To forget her was to forget the world. Each street I drove through I saw us at some point in time. Moments and touch, passion and genuine interest, now loss and blankness. I saw the fellow sometime later, short and plain, barely her height with an obvious and practiced bravado. They were holding hands at a party and when they started kissing with their chests touching and I'd never felt so far away from anyone before. The flatness I felt after that never really went away. The dull hum grew slowly from year to year, and after the death of my parents it was omnipresent, in all things and people. The void drifted into every aspect of my—

"Mark how are you?" she asks, slowly running her index finger up and down the champagne flute in her hand.

"You always were the only one to call me by my name," I say to her.

"It still baffles me that everyone calls you Indie," she replies.

Her eyes look at me with a practiced interest. In them is a blend of our old familiarity blanketed by the reality of new situations and new maturity. I look away briefly, unable to hold her gaze.

"A name is just a title."

"Are you going to go into a long-winded narrative about names and titles?" Amy says, still playing with her glass.

"No," I reply, looking at my feet.

She is wearing a dark blue hourglass dress that fits her form exquisitely with a cut by the shoulders showing the beginnings of cleavage.

"Someone is calling me," I say, waving at Ed.

"Okay," Amy replies, walking away.

Ed sees me wave and raises his palms upward while shrugging his shoulders. He mouths the words *what's up?* I stroll quickly past him and he gives me a concerned look and I go back into the bathroom, but not after taking another drink from a waiter, a Mojito I think. I take two of the Adderal, gulp the drink and splash my face with water. Back outside, I see Ed talking to Delano and Jazzy T and I walk back to my original seat, which has been vacated by the mysterious older white guy and Brittany is nowhere to be seen. Alaine gives me a friendly nod and the Dj announces the fashion show is starting. I squirm in my seat, continuously looking behind me to see where Amy is sitting, but I don't see her. Most people are seated now and the lights dim and a few skinny girls wearing different versions of the shirt reading "KINGSTON BUCK" walk out, nipples pressing adamantly through the thin fabric of the t-shirts. Then they come out again in alternate outfits, all with a hint of a silver motif to everything. My heart is racing as I look at them, thinking about Amy's eyes and the sexy dress she's wearing. I have a solid erection and I'm watching the models come and go, while they play an old Avicii track. One of the girls is stunning, with jet black skin, Grace Jones cheekbones and the ample legs and arms of the genetically superior. I lean over Alaine's lap and grab another drink from a waiter and swallow it quickly, getting lost in the music but my heart still races and I get up and walk to the back of the establishment, where I see Junior Gong with a fitted cap pulled low over his eyes surrounded by men with thick locks in an equally relaxed vibe. I see Ed walking through the lobby and ask him if he has any coke and he smiles, patting my palm. I go back to the bathroom and take a quick hit, splashing my face with water again. My face looks very calm, despite the maelstrom raging in my mind.

"Everyone is going to Gravity for the after party," Ed says, surveying the audience.

"I will see you there," I reply, rubbing my nose.

The audience is applauding and Connie does her walk down the catwalk with the models and takes a bow. Before I leave I give her eight thousand dollars and take three shirts and a cap that reads "TUNUP" and head back to the car, but not before seeing Amy with her arms interlocked with a man I'd never seen before. I get a flash of her stomach, how flat and smooth it was, and images of her in bikinis and my mouth all over her tanlines after a day in the sun in Negril. I go back into the car and look through the windshield as people spill out of the establishment, walking to European car after European car. Ed walks out with the girl with the giant ass. He is laughing with her as if he has known her forever and I see her giggling with ninety percent sincerity. I doubt she knows he is wearing a Tom Ford jacket.

"Fuck her," I say for no reason and turn on the radio.

I pull out of the parking lot, nod at the attendant who doesn't care that I've lost my parking ticket, and drive out onto the main road, heading towards Gravity.

Chapter Three

I'm praying at the wheel as I drive in a cloud of blurry vision, relishing the fading sensation of the wine on my tongue, and the images of the women I'd seen earlier. Seeing Amy had given me a slight jolt, but it is almost gone. The radio is painfully loud and the windows are all the way up. My ears burn with the need for release, but I listen to the garbled concoctions of some music producer most likely labeled as a "genius" as I career around roads and dodge men selling boxes of donuts. The streets blister in a ripple of colour. Somewhere I hear music in between the quick pause of dead air on the radio, rock steady music from a car opposite mine. I honk long and hard at a taxi that keeps pulling to the side of the road without warning or indication. The engine roars as the radio and the horn join the histrionic melody. I'm driving a little too fast and I know this, but my mind is clear and open. The night is filled with dark things; dark bodies, dark buildings, dark streets and dark intentions. I pull up to a stoplight near Trafalgar road and buy five boxes of donuts from a man wearing pink pants and a matching cap dotted with rhinestones. I let him keep the change. I put the cap with "TUNUP" embroidered on it on my head, and eat three donuts in rapid succession. They are almost stale, but the red, sweet centers still connect with my taste buds as they always do. I'm also thinking about the end of things. The inevitability of ending, the distinct reality floating over everyone's head, the feeling of non-feeling that is choking me. I'm thinking about my parents, and the form they've taken now. Ethereally floating in some cosmic chamber are they? Or nothing at all, scattered atoms in a jar stuffed into a wall at a church in Half Way Tree? Everything can be diminished into nothing. Men stand tall and are broken by injury and sickness, they freefall out of life as quickly as they enter it, and so did they. What were their thoughts adrift at sea with nothing around them but the cold water and the even colder reality of what was happening? Foolishly I had thought adults were invincible beings, unable to feel what I felt. Age, I believed created strength and unusual resilience to things, an ascended process that pushed us into immortality. I idle by a stoplight, eating another donut, and see a huge video Billboard advertising life insurance dance with brightly coloured computer graphics. My mind drifts away as I go back into the past, into the middle of a memory that seems impossible.

Twin lightning bolts flashed with the brilliance of the sun, striking the ground a few feet from where I was standing. I laughed. I was five, and unaware that death by lightning involves mind-numbing pain which leaves the smell of burnt flesh in the air. When the lighting struck the ground again, I laughed more. I thought the sky was playing with me. There had never been lightning like that since in Kingston, and it was one of the few times I remember my mother grabbing me and running inside the house, as the sky overhead spun in a dark mess, as leaves and paper flew through the sky like migrant birds.

I rarely saw my mother out of her work clothes in the evening; that simple women's suit that varied between grey and dark grey, her glasses resting on her nose as she sat in the kitchen drinking a glass of wine (or the entire bottle) before retreating into the bedroom where my father never was. Each night I would hear his Benz pull into the driveway well after one in the morning. More often than not he would pat me on the shoulder if I was playing video games or reading, stinking of rum and sex. There was no way for me to truly know what his scent was at the time of course. So used was I to his routines and smells and touches that I didn't understand a man smelling too sweet has been in the arms of a perfumed woman, or that a man sweating rum has been drinking too much. But that was the reality of who my father was to me. Tall and handsome with the sharp eyes and the constant smile, the low, controlled voice and the fear of nothing. One of these nights he came in far more wobbly than usual, roaming through the kitchen for something to eat. In the middle of trying to make a sandwich with a fresh set of Ginzu knives he'd received on a trip to Miami, he cut his arm and two fingers. Blood was everywhere, and the dark liquid dripped onto the counter as my father kept trying to make the sandwich. I ran to my mother's room, pounding on the door. She nonchalantly came out in a silk robe and walked downstairs. Without saying anything, she stopped my father from making his sandwich, stopped his bleeding cuts using paper towels and bandages, then went back upstairs. *This must be invincibility,* my mind said.

On another occasion at a barbeque, some of the men folk decided to play soccer on the road. While I romped with a few other kids in that neighbourhood, running through their massive yard I heard a commotion at the front. My father had fallen to the ground badly and his hand was broken. It hung by his side, the broken bone pressing against the skin at a strange angle. Everyone hovered around him, helping him up, while my mother pulled the Benz around, but he was laughing as if nothing happened, even after we went to the hospital and he received a cast. That hospital was not a fond memory. A nurse with hands like porridge had held me firmly there more than once when I received my yearly inoculation as a child. The syringe had looked like all things painful as she held it up, her body tall and broad, my little frame unable to resist the grip she held me in. That needle had pierced the muscle in my shoulders and left me crying for an hour. Such pain! Such fear! Things an adult would never feel.

The car tires screech as I pull into a gas station and park beside a grey van. I need a chocolate snack. Catch is the choice I make. I buy five of them and a bottle of water, some nuts and a copy of the day's paper. The headline reads "MINISTER MUST GO" and the byline has some information about a government minister using funds from a non-profit organization to buy a new home for himself. I sit in the car, eating one of the candy bars and sip on the bottle of water. Another Range Rover pulls into the station and parks opposite to mine. It is the same colour and tint. No one exits the vehicle. It could be me in that car, I think, staring back at myself in a bizarre display of parallel reality. Since the age of ten I'd thought about parallel universes. In my mind's eye I saw seven versions of myself. One was tall and thin, two looked very similar and one was broad and muscular. The other three I couldn't see clearly because they were standing behind the other four. They were perched on a cloud in the sky, smiling and waving. It was a comic book that spoke of parallel universes to me; about other selves and other realities. It made me think of a complex existence, one with endless outcomes and dualities. Like Mr. Fantastic and a host of other superheroes constantly embattled in a struggle for inter-dimensional consistency, I said I too must be a fragment of an endless and infinite universe.

I eat two more of the Candy bars and some of the nuts, but still no one leaves the Range Rover facing mine. I feel it baiting me with its similarity. I feel its driver watching me with his or her anonymity. The red wrapping on the candy bar paper reminds me of the night I saw a blood red sky and thought the world was ending. It is a natural phenomenon, my mother had said. At the time I didn't know what phenomenon meant, but it sounded like the verbal precursor to an alien invasion. This was when some work had been going on the premises to add two new rooms at the rear of the house. I went in there once at night in the dark, touching a light switch that had no plastic casing. As I lightly touched the exposed metal, electricity hit my body with a slap, sending me to the floor. I lay there in fright. I knew I wasn't invincible. The man who was responsible for the electric wiring, during the time that the area was a mess of blocks dust, and thick black wires had come to me one afternoon. His skin was dark brown and his face covered with flecks of tiny moles. There was a black, mean-looking machine with several wires running through it.

"Don't ever touch that," he had said. "It will kill you."

I knew death was a place of no return. I was nine when he told me that. I realized what death was. I imagined my father never coming back from work, never seeing my mother in the kitchen in her work suit, and never coming home. That day I ran into my mother's arms and wept. I asked her if I was going to die. Yes, she had replied. We all die.

And now they were gone.

I finish the bottle of water and feel like having a Ginger Beer, but I decide to leave the gas station. The Range Rover is still parked in the lot, its driver still mysterious and anonymous. I go down the road slowly because Gravity is close by now, and I pull into the parking lot, slowing down to let Assassin, Baby Cham and two other guys walk pass the front of the car. Today I can't get VIP parking because its full and I park near the front, beside a person in a white Honda CRV mysteriously chatting in the car with Tristan, who's Audi is nowhere to be seen. I step out of the vehicle and walk slowly through the parking lot towards the entrance. The Kingston chill is high now, and despite wearing a thin H&M sports jacket and a cotton undershirt, I'm feeling the tickle of the wind on my arms, causing light goose bumps to form under the fabric. A person with a familiar face waves at me—some dude from high school—and I see the stunning model from the fashion show walking with two of her friends towards a giant SUV where Usain Bolt and Christopher Martin stand with ten other people. Ed's S500 is parked in VIP and I smirk for no real reason as I walk towards the entrance of the club, where the bouncer nods and me and let's me in, then stops a guy coming in after me who's wearing a cap similar to mine and says to him he can't wear caps in the club.

Inside is a massive dedication to the interior of clubs worldwide. There is space for people to amble about while they drink and engage in deleterious behaviour, dim lights and deep corners for people that don't want to be seen, and obvious VIP booths for those who do want to be seen. Ed waves me into his booth where he's sitting with ten people including Shaggy, a reggae artiste from France, Gyptian's tour manager, the head of a large private equity firm, the girl with the big ass from the fashion show and a few extremely attractive girls who are in their last year of school at the University of the West Indies. Bottles of rum and champagne dot the table and our server walks over to me.

"If you need anything please let me know," she says.

Her name is Maria and I've seen her a million times but there is no recognition in her eyes, only the sensation that I must be someone to know these people, and therefore have become more than the blurry visage of whoever I was to her before. I send her on a meaningless errand to get cranberry chasers even though there are three full jugs of cranberry already on the table for the VIPs.

"This is Sherene," Ed says to me while giving her a pinch on the shoulder.

Sherene is the girl Ed had eyed earlier at the fashion launch. Her face is cute but I don't find much about her remarkable, other than a mysterious tattoo of a dove on her left wrist. She extends a hand and takes mine carefully in hers as her eyes probe mine, weighing my relative value.

"I like your hat," she says. "I was going to get one myself, but I decided to get it later."

"I know Connie," Ed replies. "I'll set it up now."

Sherene waves her hand as if to say no, but Ed is already on his phone and standing up, scanning the horizon. He waves to someone and they come over, exchanging hushed words. The person is a young man I don't recognize, with a flat, serious face. He nods vigorously as Ed talks to him, and then he darts into the thick of the crowd. Ed sits down and smiles at Sherene.

"Done and done," he says. "I won't have you lacking anything on such an interesting night."

"Thanks," Sherene replies, gracefully sipping on a drink in front of her.

"TUN UP!" I shout to everyone and no one while pointing to my hat, getting me a smile and a nod from Shaggy.

A few feet away, I see the man wearing the gabardine making a fuss about not being let into our area. He walks off in a huff, going towards the terrace outside. I take a quick scan of the crowd, noticing mostly the same people from the launch, plus more reggae artistes, models and girls that should be in their dorm rooms studying for exams. Ed is working on Sherene in his usual manner, all self-aggrandizement and lack of tact. As usual, it is working.

"It is such a pain to look for a good boat captain," Ed says to Sherene, who nods in response as if she is used to hearing such things. I'm usually mildly entertained by this spectacle, because Sherene's ginormous ass has some capital, but not *that much*. I knew Ed was gauging in his mind how fast he would sleep with her, and I would no doubt hear the gristly details of her sexual proclivities sometime soon.

"What sort of boat do you have?" Sherene says with what I must say sounds like genuine interest or oscar worthy acting.

"Boats are best seen and not heard," Ed said emphatically, waving his hands.

"I thought that phrase related to children," I say, feeling slightly nervous as I see a girl that looks like Amy walk past Bounty Killer's table.

"A good boat," Ed starts to say, his face gaining an immediate seriousness, "Is like a child."

I leave the twin actors for a moment and go to the terrace on the second floor of the club. A girl I know who is also in the fashion industry as a makeup artiste is standing by the upstairs bar. After saying a quick hello to her, I turn to her friend. The friend is tall and has a look of elegance, but her energy is fidgety.

"Good evening," I say.

"Evening," she replies curtly.

"Are you also a designer like Jenna?" I ask, waving at a bartender.

"No, I work for Condé Nast," she replies, not looking at me.

The bartender gives me a rum and coke and I take a quick sip.

"Wow that sounds interesting," I reply.

"You know Condé Nast?" she asks, still not looking at me.

"How can one not be familiar with the company that publishes Vanity Fair, Vogue, W, Wired and GQ?"

"I see," the girl replies, still not looking at me.

Jenna is chatting on the phone to someone, not caring much about our conversation. The girl's potential elegance is overriding the reality of what I'm seeing unfolding.

"So miss Condé Nast, what area do you work in?"

"Fashion."

"Lovely. Men's or women's?"

She shoots me a dirty look.

"Women's fashion," she says dryly.

I tell the bartender to give her a drink and she orders a Mai Tai. She says something to Jenna after getting the drink, then turns back to me.

"Thanks for the drink," she says without a smile.

"So what area of fashion do you focus on?" I ask, shaking the ice cubes in my glass.

"Uh, all areas," she says, her eyes looking left and right.

"All areas eh? So I guess you have pretty strong opinions on fashion?"

"Pretty much," she replies, taking a garish pink umbrella out of her glass.

"Do you think Daniella Westbrook was almost responsible for the demise of Burberry?"

"Who?"

"Are you of the opinion Jamaican women should wear more diaphanous clothing?"

"Uh, sure, why not."

"Oh so they don't wear it enough then?"

"I guess."

"There are three women in the club tonight wearing outfits with Dollman sleeves. Isn't that appalling?"

She nods in reply.

"Just once," I say, "I want to take my Birkin out on the town."

She pauses in the middle of sipping her drink, and looks at me directly for the first time.

"You own a Birkin bag?"

I don't reply and walk back downstairs and into the throng. Ed's booth has even more people now, jockeying for attention with the celebrities and sneaking free liquor. I leave after noticing a man drinking beer from a goblet. I go to the bathroom and splash my face with water, as a man stands beside me and constantly preens his hair in light strokes. He is of mixed ethnicity, handsome and possesses an effortless air of arrogance. After seeing the fifteenth pass of his hand over his head I go into one of the stalls, do another hit of the coke Ed gave me and go back into the party. The music is good, and I see the man in the gabardine near a corner. I don't feel sorry for him until I notice he has a Balenciaga tote bag and I get him into VIP. I don't follow him in and stand near a wall and buy a Mai Tai but I don't drink it. I blink my eyes as strobe lights kick my retinas, and the crowd erupts into a cacophony of positive cheers when a Vybz Kartel song blasts over the airwaves. Amy appears in the distance, her eyes scanning the horizon, concerned. I know the concern isn't for me.

Her expression reminds me of a girl from college. Her name is unimportant. With my eyes closed, in my mind, I leave the club momentarily. The girl was a townie, a redhead with freckles on her shoulders that I'd been exclusively seeing for three months. One night she said to me with tears in her eyes that she slept with someone else. I took the news in silence. The dude was some idiot rugby player with no personality named Biff. That weekend I took a flight to Miami and did nothing but sit by the beach and watch the blue green waves lap playfully against the white shore. I stuffed my body with expensive pita bread sandwiches and margaritas and focused on the horizon. Things were so flat and calm I felt like writing a poem in that moment, but I didn't. In the stillness of the dark night that followed, I meet a girl named Ariana. We made love in my hotel room and watched reruns of *I Love Lucy* for the rest of the weekend. I never saw her again. I am not sure why a girl I will never see again named Ariana replaces the memory of the redhead's name. All I remember is what happened on the Monday when I spoke to the redhead again, and gone were her tears of regret. Her attitude had shifted into something else, a steely resolve that what she had done was right, that it was my fault she took another guy in her mouth and god knows where else. Her expression lacked any concern or caring. She was void as I was void in Miami, staring at me with as much emptiness as an immeasurable sea view. This was what I felt from Amy as well, more nothingness and lack of concern.

Candice strolls over to me oddly, and rests a hand on my shoulder. She leans forward to kiss me on the cheek but I move my head away and take her hand and walk with her outside.

"Cliff is such an asshole," she says to me as we walk past the bouncer and through the parking lot.

"Assholes are everywhere, aren't they?" I ask, as we walk towards my vehicle.

"I just needed a little help replacing my iPhone screen and he kept saying no," she says with genuine annoyance.

"The gall of this fellow," I reply as we enter the backseat of the car

"Yes, I'm tired of them," she says while undoing my pants.

"The music was good though," I remark, slipping the left strap of her dress down her shoulder and past her elbow.

I press the autostart key and the air conditioning trickles through the vents.

"Oh, why do you want the air on? It is so cold outside," Candice says, struggling to pull my belt from my pants.

As I kiss her shoulders and rub her thighs I reply, "The cold keeps things sharp."

I lean back as she expertly blows me with equal parts voracity and sensuality. Normally this gets me off, but I'm too wired and after a few minutes I lay her down, hiking up her skirt and slipping off her exquisite pair of black lace Dolce and Gabbana panties. In the corner of my eye, I see the short man she was with at the fashion show far in the distance with a phone on his ear. I time my thrusts to each *vmmmm, vmmmm, vmmmm* her phone makes as the guy dials her. Candice comes in a strange mixture of moans and growls and leaves the car quickly, but not before taking one of my candy bars. I sit in the backseat for a while, liking the prickly feeling of tiny beads of sweat on my forehead because of the cool air swirling around in the car. I'm hungry again, and I decide to leave the after party, not before noticing Candice left her panties on the backseat. My phone vibrates a few times as she calls me to retrieve them, but I don't answer as I'm already driving up the road to a place where I can get something hot and fried as I think to myself, maybe I am traumatized. I hit the gas and feel the engine gleefully pickup speed as the car rockets towards a stoplight. Fifty feet away and I see it change to amber. Still going, I see the light turn red three seconds before I blaze through it. No cars drift into my path, and there is no sickening crunch of metal on metal, the explosive hit of an airbag on my face and the possibility of several casualties. I'm way past the stop light now with the engine howling at the sky with no end in sight.

Chapter Four

I'm on auto-pilot, awake and clear. The day before me is filled with predictability of structure and form. Soft clouds make their sacrosanct pilgrimage across their ever-azure plains. Looking out on the horizon I can see it all, all the restaurants and shopping malls, the main streets and the highways, the after party locations and the various boroughs people live in. I can see out towards the harbour where massive tankers bring in shipped goods, the stretch of the highway leading out of town towards Portmore, and the thin strip of the blue sea in the distance. The smell of grass and the trees around me feels ubiquitous, like the light sensation of the sun hitting me with its luminous gaze. I didn't take any of the Ambien the night before and I haven't slept since I went to Gravity. Because of this there was nothing much for me to do except stand in a cold shower for a while, as the shower radio blasted rock music in my ears. The cold made me feel numb, but nothing more.

I walk in a bathrobe to the den, feeling the weight of my man's body grip the robe tightly, a robe that barely fit me only years before I glimpse myself in a nearby mirror, the face and legs far removed from a time before, and I drift into the past. I remember the walls of my high school, tall and ever present at the time, blocking the outside world I know. Back then, spending my days posturing in my khaki uniform and thinking about nothing in particular, the outside world with the din of traffic I'd hear drift into the cafeteria windows at lunchtime was merely the noise of people I didn't know doing things I didn't care about. The *outside world* wasn't a thing. There were just my days within those walls, gallivanting with friends and the dynamics of a teenage life mostly without worry. Sometimes there were school trips to various places. The National Gallery of art downtown, or some interschool conference where we learned about things like brands and trademarks. There were the steps out into the world for art competitions where kids scrawling terrible pieces of art on sheets of cartridge paper received accolades for nothing more than the poor execution of an idea. I had tried entering one of these competitions, to draw a poster for an environmental cause. The day I decided to make that piece of art, my eyes gleamed as I looked upon the blank sheet in front of me. There in my mind's eye was the most beautiful work of art ever. On it was a hyper realistic portrayal of a junk-yard dotted with the carcasses of once vibrant animals. There were puddles of stagnant liquid and cars that covered in rust, thick ridges of dried mud stuffed with the waste of a hundred years. Cans marked "radioactive" with hairline cracks leaking green ooze from them were everywhere, sending rippling chemical waves into the air. The real drawing was of course, quite different. It was a terrible mess of squiggly lines and poorly drawn animals. But it was part of that time of purity, and seeing beauty in things such as blank sheets of paper and competitions. This I realized, was my first true taste of failure. My lack of ability stung me. I was angry, my vision hadn't born any fruit, I would not be receiving any accolades. In the world I am in now, the present moment, failure is in the face at every turn one makes. There are no illusions because there is no-where to escape those whom you have seen and who have seen you. The broken dinner dates, the elusive lies and elaborate dodges are all revealed by the long arm of time and coinci-dence. Where else can one go other than one's hometown? But often a hometown becomes saturated with the familiarity of it's borders, the veritable hamster cage with everyone running on the same treadmill sweaty and pungent, looking forwards and never behind even as bodies collide into one another and peo-ple get trampled as the wheels keep on turning. Maybe this is how it is supposed to be, this sharp perspective, this blank outlook.

I sit on my couch and flip through *Annie Leibovitz At Work* and consider buying a digital camera. Perhaps I could roam the streets of Kingston and capture its "essence" with the right equipment and dedication. My name would soar throughout the hallways of the elite as the go-to man for projects because I have the eye for the task. I would be a man of the people, unafraid of the street, unafraid of the message because I was the messenger. My outfits would consist mainly of black clothing and well-knit beanies that people wouldn't know cost over a hundred dollars. My camera would be my constant companion, more so than my girlfriend, who would be a rugged artist from a wealthy family that tossed away the oppressive shackles of her family's corporate legacy. She would passionately speak to me about political issues and read her poetry to me, spend endless amounts of money on her acrylics and canvases, her trips to the country and meaningless artistic residencies where people would peck at her whim and fancy, saying she had *je ne sais quoi* and her work was so *avant garde*. Our lovemaking would be brutally passionate, filled with arguments and somewhere in my collection of images, would be a picture of her, in the bed sheets looking at me with a furtive expression that holds neither anger or love. This picture would be framed in my apartment, which would be threadbare and lacking of a sensitive touch. A man of the people cannot have a sensitive touch. But there would be intelligence in that apartment. There would be books by Frantz Fanon and Nietzsche, Tolstoy and Dostoevsky. Pictures of Marcus Garvey, Nelson Mandela and Hunter S. Thompson would stare at me from odd locations like the kitchen door, my bathroom mirror and from the ceiling of my bedroom. I'd host dinner parties where everyone would eat couscous and vegetarian meat substitutes and we'd talk about our favourite novels and I'd say how much *Anna Karenina* impacted me, but not as much as *The Enigma of Arrival* by V.S Naipaul. Someone would no doubt talk about a pop novel, some fat Stephen King tome or a Sidney Sheldon classic, then an argument would ensue about Ralph Ellison versus Alexander Theroux and then everyone would smoke weed, the cool guy with the long locks would pull out his guitar and we'd all start singing some tired Bob Marley songs late into the night. Then my artistic girlfriend would come over, smelling like black soap, wearing her typical linen pants and hemp shirts and her eyes would be red and she'd be hanging with a guy that I know she sleeps with sometimes, but I wouldn't care because I'd delude myself into thinking I am that open-minded, that I understand sexual passion is a thing that creative people intrinsically possess, and sexual expression of said passion is a necessary conduit for one's growth in any journey of self-discovery. I'd mask my jealousy in weird arguments that have nothing to do with things of any merit, and instead of making love to her I'd retreat into small bedroom I converted into a darkroom and develop photos late into the night as I focus on the real matters of the world. The tone of my images would be my ultimate focus as I'd use them to try and tell people the right messages, the message that the power of the mind is held in the slight grasp of a man's ability to let people know clearly what he sees. I'd give talks to students about finding a pure passion and following it no matter what. I'd talk about not selling out to do huge campaigns for companies like Pepsi and Nokia. I will discuss the Vogue photo shoot I did and chuckle at the rumours that I was linked to a supermodel based in Paris. I will keep going, creating my images and follow my passion through several disastrous relationships, fluctuations in my weight and temperament. But I don't own a camera, and I can never be this person.

I've tried only once to explain how I feel about the world. It was to an old friend back in town for a week that invited me to play pool at a bar in New Kingston. The gap between periods of seeing someone you have vague familiarity with tends to amplify the regurgitation of familiar data. Facts from years back float to the surface of relevant reality snapping into focus the firm knowledge that this person does not actually know you very well. Either way, we were driving to this bar, the kind blanketed in darkness and filled with open-air couches and an endless supply of disgruntled waitresses. We ordered some drinks. A song played on through the speakers, 'Jeremy' by Pearl Jam and we sat there for a while as we waited on the order to arrive.

"I feel like I want to die," I said flatly.

His eyes widened and a stern look appeared on his face. He was a round faced Chinese fellow everyone called Khan because he looked like Kublai Khan.

"What the fuck do you mean you want to die?" he said.

I explained that I felt no inspiration to do anything, and that I was being slowly choked by the predictable paradigms of

Kingston. As if on cue, a few of his friends said hello, tall light-skinned fellows flanked by attractive dark skinned girl with jaded eyes. These were girls who would never say hello to me, or even see me beyond anything except a person sitting in the shadows.

"Everybody bomboclaat life has a purpose," Khan said to me, wagging a thick finger in my direction.

"I—I'm not sure," I stammered, feeling the ice in my drink burn my gums.

"Do you know what the only constant in life is bredrin?" he asked.

"What?"

He leaned forward slightly, his small eyes almost hidden in the vast width of his face. "Uncertainty. It is the only thing that you can truly rely on. This means that pointlessness is a virtue. Everything in this life, our goals our direction is all fucking meaningless. You know what you are?"

"Tell me," I replied.

"You are a fucking fluctuation of time and space. That is it. You are an expression of energy."

"So my reality has no meaning?" I asked.

"Damn right. Everything is energy. This universe, me and you we are all energy. If you know this and accept it you can live moment to moment without too much mental hassle. Right now because of this outlook, I can set goals and plan for the future, etcetera."

"Didn't you say all those things were meaningless?" I replied.

"Meaningless relative to the acceptance of what you are, just a fragment of some boundless fucking energy that you can't even begin to fathom the size or scope of. Don't add a bunch of bullshit to a scenario that didn't even have to bring you into this reality."

Khan was probably right, but he didn't live here anymore. Khan lives in Miami where he is involved in artiste management and does show bookings. Khan is also the kind of fellow who is already drunk by five in the afternoon, meaning whatever I said to him was lost in shattered brain cells. His life is outside of the Kingston bubble. I think about the night before, wondering why I sped through that red light. Recklessness is a symptom perhaps, but in the blanket of my malaise what is a symptom, really. There is no predictability in recklessness. Randomness is the last refuge of a man that knows the cards before they are dealt. I slip off the robe and sit naked on a Naoto Fukusawa chair. I flip open my Macbook Air and open Microsoft Word. I'm taking a film studies class, and I need to write an essay on an influential fictional figure and why they are meaningful.

> There is not person quite as complex in as Bruce Wayne. Both hero and antihero, his personality and the fuel that makes him push towards constant perfection is relative to his trauma, the death of his parents. Rooted in thi

My phone rings and I answer it.

"Mark? This is Uncle John."

"Longtime no speak," I say, running a finger along the outer edges of the laptop.

"We need to have lunch today," he says.

In the background I can hear the shuffling of papers and someone speaking behind him in a low voice.

"I don't think I can do that today, I'm working on an essay."

"What kind of essay," he asks.

"I'm letting the world know about the true Bruce. Too often he has had inequitable things written about him in print."

"Bruce Golding?"

56

"No, Bruce Wayne."

"Mark, twelve o'clock today. We'll have Indian food."

"It's ten thirty now."

"So? You have time, I'll see you there."

He hangs up and I feel a deep, tingling familiarity. It frightens me how similar his voice sounds to my father's. The same lilt of the tongue, the way they drop their *ahs* into certain words. We'll h*ahve* Indian food today. His commands are hard to resist. In his voice I am a child again standing near my father as he demands I do something.

> The notion of a fragmented human society post-world war three is a popularly accepted notion in popular literature and film. *A brave new world*, *1984* and *The Chyrsalids* are but a few stories which have expansive prose on the subject matter. Cormac McCarthy's take is more individualistic, but still fits into the general theme of "everything done gone wrong". The idea that Bruce Wayne could "break" (psychologically) should he be the protagonist in such a scenario brings to mind the question of his resilience. In such lauded stories as *Batman: Venom* he displays remarkable adaptive abilities under the extreme duress of a highly addictive drug which gives him superhuman abilities. The manner in which he deals with this addi

I stop typing on the laptop and throw on some clothes. The light burns my eyes and I slip on dark glasses as I make the quick sojourn to Marketplace. Heat rises from the streets as young boys run around barefoot on scalding asphalt to clean windshields and women bark *Banana, Banana, hundred dollars! Banana, Banana, hundred dollars!* as they hold bags of the yellow produce in their hands. The car glides past men impervious to the heat, men walking briskly in purple long sleeved shirts with striped neckties without a dot of sweat on their foreheads. Working women in flats or oddly shaped heels trek to bus stations and vagabond students roam in packs, heading to video arcades. Hondas and Suzukis pepper the road with fumes and music, men on bikes veer dangerously into driving lanes and people consistently drive through red lights. I see Japanese tourists walking on the roadside, a Rastafarian with locks hanging almost to the ground and three men pushing an old Lada to jumpstart it. A massive white Land Rover honks at me and I don't honk back because I cannot see through the tint of the windows and wonder how they saw me. Men rush my car at a stoplight and attempt to wipe the windshield, but the car automatically turns on the wipers and one of young men shouts at me but I cannot hear him because the windows are up and I'm not a part of the hot outdoor world. I open the window and I give him five hundred dollars and he thanks me. This I know will fuel the approach to any car like mine for weeks to come. I am fueling the annoyance of drivers. The road ends and I'm pulling into Marketplace, lightly holding a parking card which I know is covered in foul germs and drive past my Uncle's Toyota Prado and park beside a VW Beetle. Beside a large black potted plant is the entrance to the restaurant. When I walk in, I look around and see my uncle sitting near the back, his large frame imposing even as he sits down. I walk over and he stands up, slightly taller than me, and shakes my hand.

"Mark, good to see you," he says.

"You too I reply," sitting down.

He hands me a menu.

"Order whatever you want," he says, glancing at his watch.

I peer over the menu briefly, and pick a few items, none of particular interest. A sleepy waiter takes our orders and walks away quickly. My uncle leans back and takes me with a look of direct assessment, his eyes bore into me unrepentantly.

"Your father would be ashamed of you, wasting your life like this," he says.

"The dead tell no tales."

He lets out a grunt and shuffles in his seat. It has been a while since I've seen him, but this is a telltale sign of him getting into one of his famous rages. He breathes out slowly.

"Mark, I just want you to do something constructive with your time," he says.

"Do you know in Japan wearing black at work can be seen as offensive because black is generally worn at funerals?"

"I'm family, you think I don't know worry about you? When's the last time you spoke to Craig?"

Craig is my cousin, whom I see every now and then around town, but rarely say hello to. He is the pompous sort of individual dripping with such privilege even I can hardly stomach a conversation with him.

"Maybe yesterday or the day before," I lie.

"Why don't you get a job?" he asks, taking a bite of his chicken.

"The working force are often referred to as plebians by the elitists. To conform to such a standard is to be labeled. I refuse to label myself as such."

"As a plebian or an elitist?" John says with a wry smirk.

"As an elitist of course," I reply.

"So you are saying you are a plebian?"

"No, I am neither plebian nor elitist, I simply am. A wise man said, 'Being must be felt, it can't be thought.'"

"Looping in Eckhart Tolle are we? I know your IQ is off the charts, but I still have a law degree and consider myself reasonably well read."

"Then you can discuss with me the perils in destroying autotrophic sources of protein for certain sea creatures," I say after eating a spoonful of curry.

"You always dodge situations with these statements. I remember your father told me it has something to do with your intelligence, some kind of defense mechanism."

"I do not dodge, I simply shuck and jive."

John leans back in his chair, his broad shoulders swallowing its back and top rail. I see the truth of his love for me in his eyes, dark brown eyes that sing my father's name in a voiceless tenor. This love does not stimulate me though I wish it would. The server returns with our food, steaming and odorous and rests it in front of us.

"Why don't you do a passion project? Maybe you could do a party like that one you did years ago. What was it? Escape?"

"Inside," I reply.

"Yes, why not try and do something like that? Or you could always try law. You know there would be a place for you at the firm. With that brain of yours I doubt it would take you as long to get through. I can put in a good word with the facul—"

"Police a chase meh, yeah dem a chase meh, but when me dip and step out dem couldn't face meh," I say.

"What are you sayin—"

"Bablyon a chase meh, but when me dip out mi lawless."

"What?"

"I don't want to do law, so I'm quoting the words of a Baby Cham song entitled 'lawless'".

John sighs.

"I'm not going to waste this meal, but please think about what I've said. If you ever need to talk to someone, I'm here."

He smiles at me, and I see my father again in his face, full of life, tall and ever present. I simply nod, and we finish our meal quietly to the backdrop of clinking glasses and knives. After I leave and head back to the car, I flip open my phone and dial Andrew.

"Indie I can't talk long," he says to me, his voice filled with alternate occupations.

"This won't take long," I reply. "I think I'm going to throw another *Inside* party."

"Nice!" Andrew remarks, the tone of his voice shifting dramatically. "When are you going to have it?"

"A few days, same format. We pick a house, get some drinks and get the word out."

"Sounds like a plan, man!"

Andrew hangs up the phone and I sit there, watching a family walk by completely interested in their own lives and their pressing goal of filling their stomachs.

Chapter Five

I'm back at the party held in some parking lot in new Kingston sitting in my car. The chill is even worse today and I'm wearing a black Christopher Kane sweater, my black 'TUNUP' hat, black Cheap Monday jeans and black Jasper sneakers. I swallow some Appleton in a cup of ice, swirling it around my mouth, relishing the burn. Five young men walk by in yellow shirts that read "STATIC POOL PARTY, APRIL 28TH". Behind them three girls in cheap skirts and ugly sandals wearing the same yellow shirts hand fliers to people driving into the gate. One of them comes over to my vehicle attempting to leave a flyer on the windscreen. I turn the lights on, startling her, then wind down my window and wave 'no' to her as she tries to hand me one. The music inside is mellow dancehall music from the nineties, because it is still early, if one a.m in the morning is considered early. I leave the car and walk inside, nodding at the bouncer, saying hello. I see three people, two girls and a guy that I recognize from various parties around town and tell them about *Inside,* and how it is invite only.

"The concept is a popup party," I say to them. "Everything is free, and it's happening in the next three days."

"Wow that sounds good, I can always drink free juice," one of the young men says.

I nod and give them Andrew's number for confirmation for the list entrance. I see Eileen, a girl I went out with a while back. Eileen was of average height with wide hips and a curvy body. Her face was youthful and unwrinkled, her skin dark brown and her nose uncharacteristically straight. I'd met her on a good night, the kind that is rare for me, where I'm laughing and smiling for no reason and the people around me are coasting on energy that doesn't have anything to do with alcohol. I'd invited her out soon afterwards.

"Are you taking me on a date?" was her first question.

"I guess so," I replied with a smile in my voice.

We'd gone to a bar off Constant spring road, a little hole-in-the-wall that was quiet and reasonably private. She'd worn an attractive outfit of tight black jeans that accentuated her generous hips, a halter top with frills sewn on them that bordered on tacky but looked good, and thick-rimmed non-prescription glasses. We had drinks and chatted about life. I liked something about her smile, the way she blinked a little bit too fast, and how full her lips looked with gloss on them.

"I'm going to be a model," she said to me with a smile.

"Oh really now?" I asked.

"Yes, I'm signed to an agency and I'm wondering about how being a model will affect my life."

In my eyes she didn't look like the prototypical model. Her face could work for ad work perhaps, but with her wide hips and average height, I didn't see her going very far, but she didn't see it that way.

"I have so many things to consider," she said to me, briefly resting a hand on my shoulder. "I have to think about my nine to five job and the responsibilities that come with this new reality."

"Ah, okay," I said disinterestedly.

The conversation was light and still reasonably enjoyable, but after that night, she didn't answer any of my phone calls or text messages. Sometimes if I thought about her I would send her a message asking her if she wanted to meet up. *That's okay,* the reply would always read. The next time I saw her she was with a businessman I knew personally, a man that terrorized the social circuit by regaling women with tales of his properties in Portland and the lure of a life where all their needs are provided for. He gave me a hearty hello and introduced me to Eileen, who pretended to be meeting me for the first time, shaking my hand and saying "Indie! That's such a cool nickname. Why do people call you that?" I'd played along with the silly game, even feigning a laugh as the businessman pulled me to the side, telling me how the first night they went out he had sex with her in a bathroom at some Chinese restaurant.

Eileen stands near a table filled with liquor bottles, her face unsmiling and marked with worry. The man sitting at the table with her is an older man with a rough face riddled with pock-marks. Her eyes catch mine briefly, and I walk past her and towards the bar. I say hello to a brand manager at Digicel and two of his friends visiting town from Miami, telling them about *Inside* and then I buy a bottle of Appleton and stand by a free table, passing Mary, a short slim woman I'd met at a Soca Cooler party. It was the kind of party where everyone temporarily removes some of their Kingston shackles, the borders between various social groups blur and new connections are born. We'd spoken by the food tent, and she told me she liked bands like The Cranberries and surprisingly, Fleetwood Mac. I told her I thought *Rumours* was an excellent album and she agreed, telling me her favourite track was "Gold Dust Woman". She had a nice smile, an endearing, delicate face complimented by a moving, interesting energy. I took her to my cooler and we made drinks, talking about the lack of rock bands in Kingston and how great the party was. Without any prodding from me, she danced with me as the soca hits played, rubbing my thighs playfully, seemingly without a need for the original group she came with. We exchanged numbers and I was smiling as I left, curious to learn more about her. She didn't answer any phone calls or texts and the next time I saw her she was with a friend of mine from high school, a weird fidgety fellow who was on his third attempt at Law school. I said hello to her, still coasting on the memories our night of Rock and Roll diatribes and jaunted forays into interesting topics. After I had come over, she said a cordial hello and squeezed my hand. It was not a friendly squeeze, but the kind that let's a person know that they should walk away. I acquiesced in this moment, raising my plastic cup to her and the awkward fellow in a salute, and went back to wherever I was standing.

She sees me and opens her mouth as if to say hello, but I'm talking to the guy beside her, Ricardo, a photographer who specializes in bikini photography and tell him about *Inside,* telling him to bring friends and hot girls. He laughs and pats me on the back, turning to introduce me to Mary, but I'm already walking back to my table. I run into a DJ I know tell him about the party and he nods, processing a virtual calendar in his mind.

"Oh! *Inside!* Yeah man, I'll be there. You should have brought that party back a long time ago!"

He disappears in a cloud of positive energy and I go to the table, fixing a strong drink and high five a girl who does promotional work at events I sometimes visit. When she moves out of my vision, I see Valerie, a last year student at the University of the West Indies who is originally from Spain. She is tall, with smooth Mediterranean skin always polished in a seamless tan. Her hair is normally pulled back into a tight ponytail, but tonight it is down past her shoulders, resting on a sparkling silver top with flecks of black adorning its surface to compliment her black skirt. I'd met her at a Latin night mixer one of my Embassy friends had invited me to, loving the sound of her Spanish voice and the way her hazel eyes looked at me as I danced salsa and samba with her. She had a powerful confidence and an insistent energy that made her seem much taller than her five feet eight inches of height.

"I get what I want," she told me as we stood near the lobby of the restaurant that doubled as the Latin night location. I wiped sweat off my brow and smiled as she said this.

"What is it that you want?" I had asked, my eyes filled with innuendo.

She rested a long index finger on her lips, kissing it lightly.

"It's a secret," she told me before taking me into a corner and giving me a light kiss on the neck.

At that time, the promise of being with her excited me. I liked her smell, her eyes and the unfamiliar territory of our cultural differences. In the parking lot that night, as I was leaving a guy I saw around sometimes approached me. He was short, with the uneasy gleam of something dark in his eyes.

"I saw you chatting to Valerie," he said.

"And?"

"You throw that party called *Inside* yeah? I know you are probably a hype guy and what not, but be careful. The girl has a... *reputation.*"

I had ignored the strange little man with his weird eyes, only to learn from several sources that he was correct. Valerie was apparently a notorious maneater, unapologetic in her activities as she bedded men from all walks of life in her student apartment. I heard about her hooking up with businessmen, street vendors, dancers, reggae artistes and producers. She had even gone home with a fellow the night I'd met her at the Latin mixer. I tried to trust the feeling I had inside me in the days that followed. That little touch of intrigue and curiosity that made me think about her eyes and her hair. Sometime later, she saw me at a bar, hugged me and gave me a wet kiss on the cheek, asking why I hadn't called her. I was frigid in my response, asking her why she was interested in me if she was sleeping with other guys.

"I like you a lot," she had said to me, pausing as if that statement was supposed to be enough for me to dive into bed with her and her man harem.

My lack of response warranted nothing from her, as she immediately went to the bar and started chatting up an old guy three steps away from death's door.

Valerie looks older and worn as she stands briefly by herself at the entrance to the party, pulling out her cell phone. She looks up, and waves at someone, a tall man obviously not from Jamaica, and they head to the bar. I take another drink, ignoring the requests of a girl I don't know beside me trying to get a free drink, and glimpse the fiery red Honda of a popular reggae artiste named Flame pull into a reserved parking space. Soon after he strolls in at a quick clip, followed by an entourage of five men and three women, one of whom is Cynthia. Cynthia is a truly attractive woman, with clear dark skin, a sharp, well-constructed face and a well proportioned body. She has an unusual sort of confidence, which is the main thing I remembered after I met her at an album release party. I saw her a few times afterward, only to learn she was obsessed with her ex-boyfriend who was an aging Reggae artiste that spent most of his year traveling in Europe.

"All he does is just fuck these white girls," she would say to me, always calling me late at night.

The references to him and his life were pathological. Her eyes would take on a strange expression and the rants would proceed unabated for minutes on end. Then a song would play on the radio if we were driving, or I'd say something and she'd snap back to attention. Her interest in me was relative to driving her to events or taking her to dinner. We had one or two brief sexual encounters doused in awkwardness. Eventually she didn't answer any of my calls or texts, and then I saw an article in The Star about "Can Flame's New Girl cool him down?" The photo displayed an image of Cynthia and the artiste, holding hands and flashing million dollar smiles as they stood in some wooded area. The article said they had been seeing each other for months and finally decided to get serious. Months included the time I had been seeing her as well.

Flame and his crew walk rapidly to a far, dark corner of the parking lot opposite my direction where the men immediately begin crushing ganja in their palms and a waiter hurriedly drags a table to him and runs to get bottles of Hennessy and chasers. Cynthia stands in the group, looking sexy in a dark red dress, her eyes filled with the relaxed notion she is an obvious prize.

I feel like leaving and take the bottle of Appleton and my Pepsi chaser and head to the car, not before seeing Angela, a girl that came on to me brutally some time before. She was cute and passionate, the kind of person that liked to watch Disney cartoons and cook. Her mind was halfway between being in the corporate world and being a complete artist, which is why I guess she chose to work in film production. She was always busy, always on a shoot, but often called me in the early hours of the morning, telling me she wanted to see me, that she was bored and needed attention. I'd fallen for these antics, thinking that her sentiments were real, but then I'd spoken to Andrew about her and he told me that she knew about my background and that she had just broken up with her boyfriend and wanted somewhere new to live. I was shocked at the time. With her I had sex that could set asbestos aflame. She had been reeling me slowly into both into her vagina and her mind, cementing a sense of rapid commitment with memories of nights watching *Duck Tales* and eating Bigfoot snacks.

The car is still cool as I sit inside. I close my eyes and turn on the air conditioning, feeling it tickle my nose. I drop the extra bottle of rum at the foot of the front passenger seat and turn on the car engine. There is light traffic on the road coming into the venue and I drive past men selling pots of soup outside who shout *Elder! Elder! Get a cup no?* The men in vests who assist people in parking on the road come up to the car window, asking me for handouts despite knowing I was parked inside. I don't wind down the window, and I don't turn on the radio. I drive to the nearby Terra Nova Casino and sit at a table alone, watching ESPN sportscenter play muted on the screen and I wonder why there are no closed captions displayed. Inside is cold, and "Peaches and Cream" is playing over the airwaves when to my left I see three people walk in, women of means in expensive skirts and heels out on a night away from their husbands. One of them is Kayla, whom I'd met at a charity 5K run a few years ago, where she had complimented me on my physique and kept insisting I meet her friends. I did, and after the race we all went out for drinks and I wondered why she had invited me there because her body language was devoid of anything sexual, in fact I didn't find her that attractive but I was idle and after running I'm more charged sexually because of the increased blood flow in my body. She kept buying me drinks and talking about life and we hung with her friends Stan, Edward and Stacey. Stan was weird and kept talking about the race and how his body felt, until it dawned on me that Stan was gay and Kayla was trying to broker something with me. Once I saw she was trying to hook me up with his guy I left the place, annoyed and went home.

The women drift to the blackjack tables, where they giggle and whip out thousands of dollars to buy credits. A voice calls my name, and I see Adam. He is a short, white Jamaican fellow with a gently subdued, gregarious energy. He has a flat face, short low cropped hair and average features, but was a legendary cocksman. He was one of those men who had never experienced what I would call true rejection. He was the ideal in a post-colonial society stuffed with the indelicate mores of hegemony; the standard upon which other men were set and some impossibly so. A bad day for him was a bad life for others, his painful memories paled in comparison to the pain that men who looked upon him felt, as they realized that legions of women would forever have him in their minds, even if they were naked and in the throes of ecstasy with someone else. He would be hovering over the ceiling as an erotic phantasm, the ultimate provider and baby daddy, a man with the mixed virtues of down to earth Jamaicanism and the intrigue of someone originally from somewhere else, someone who didn't have the mark of ancestry involving people being beaten and raped as a cruel method of ushering them into the industrial age.

"Indie, how are you my brother?" he says with a smile.

I smile at him and offer him a drink.

"Oh thanks man, I always appreciate a good offer," he replies, sitting beside me.

I have nothing against Adam, who is incidentally named Adam Whiteman. Our histories are indelibly connected, from the days of high school when we'd play soccer after school and argue about silly things like comic books and which girls had the biggest breasts at school. But there was one day, when we took a trip to the YMCA and we were swimming in the pool. All of us were excellent swimmers, but as little boys do, we dove into the deep end in a thick throng of flailing limbs. Everyone was jostling around, jockeying for attention as chlorine burned our eyes and water roared in our ears with each descent our heads made underwater, voluntary or not. Of the thirty tiny legs kicking about in the water, one hit me full on in the stomach and I went under, choking and unable to breath. Water snaked down my nose as I gasped and gulped, convulsing in terror from my growing hysteria. Everything was a foamy vision in front of my eyes, seeing nothing but the refracted images of the other young boys gleefully swimming above me, getting obscured by the frantic oscillating of dark streaks in front of me that were my little arms. A finality started to set into my mind that I would probably die here, in the presence of all these other boys, kicked accidentally by a kid who wouldn't even remember kicking me. Things grew dark, but not before I felt a hand grab me. In the corner of my eye, it was Adam, with his then long auburn hair swirling above his head like sea snakes. He did a few powerful kicks and pulled me to the surface, screaming at some other kids to come and help. Back then scream was all we could do, with our high unbroken voices and bodies devoid of pubic hair. Two nearby fellows helped out as I coughed and sputtered back into the world of the living. I lay flat on the side of the pool, remembering the clear blue skies above me, one of the most beautiful I could remember. Then it was Adam I saw standing over me, his face over mine, playfully grinning.

"Be careful!" he had said in his little boy voice, before diving back into the water, which I soon re-entered myself.

Later, when my body started changing, and I saw a sea of large white bumps spread across the breadth of my face and a girl at school told me I looked like a dog, people laughed and called me Spotty. But Adam, despite cashing in on the capital a young white man with shoulder length hair has in high school, never called me anything. We weren't the best of friends then, but he always gave me a broad smile, a hearty hello and was always ready to play soccer after school.

As I think of days past and Adam sits sipping on his drink he turns to me and tells me about something happening at Gravity, some hush hush after party for the launch of a new Subaru SUV.

"I'm on the list plus one," he says. "We should go."

I nod quietly in reply, finishing my drink and follow his car, a dark blue Nissan Tiida throughout the winding streets and to Gravity, where we are ushered in and I see Subaru banners everywhere and mounted flat screens showing a car commercial on repeat, a commercial starring Flame driving a red vehicle into what looks like a street dance, then I see Candice, a girl who lost interest in me after she met the son of the owner of one of the island's largest pharmaceutical companies, Pauline, a dark-skinned girl with a great fashion sense who only dates white or mulatto men, Rose a musician with haunting eyes and long brown locks who people say dated Ryan Gosling but I didn't believe them, Sophie, a girl who works at the Canadian embassy who is constantly at street dances in the ghetto, Danielle, a waitress at Devon House who was bitchy to me until the proprietor gave me a free drink, Krista a banking executive that confessed to me she liked me in high school but never answered my calls and Sophia, Kim and Elaine, all law students who take their stresses out on random men on the road and are always at events like these. I take a blood red drink from a waiter that isn't wine and stand by a wall as Adam says hello to all the big wigs he knows, mentioning to them they should come to *Inside,* my private party. Everything feels smothering and I go into the bathroom and take a hit of coke in a stall and chew furiously on my last candy bar that I took from the car before I went inside the club. Drinks are free and I enjoy myself, standing inside now, near a table with people trying too hard to look cool. I recognize a girl at the table a classmate from high school who was in my Biology class. I say hello and she smiles at me, not before the girl directly beside her walks over to me.

"No, no, no," she says.

I stare blankly at her.

"No, no, no," the girl says again, walking back to the table.

I get another drink from a waiter and everybody is dancing lightly because the DJ is really good, the girl I know from high school is gyrating her hips and smiling at the same time so I tap her on the shoulder and laughingly tell her she is a bad girl. She laughs with me, but her friend grabs my arm and looks me directly in the face.

"Why don't you just FUCK OFF!" she screams.

The men around her bob and waddle like penguins from her reaction, unsure of what happened, their eyes heavy from the consumption of liquor.

"Are you insane?" I ask, looking directly at her.

The girl is attractive, but has the face of a girl repeatedly broken by men with money and free time. The girl I know from high school, Sarah, is drunk and unaware of what is unfolding. In a moment, a short broad-chested guy comes to me, resting his hand on my shoulder. I move away, letting his arm fall to his side. Ignoring whatever he is saying behind me, I go up to the terrace and have another drink, my insides burning with mixed emotions. The girl's face and actions bother me; the fire of her reaction, the complete assumption that I had no familiarity with her friend, the choked anger and dismissive energy in her voice. Adam sees me and comes over.

"You alright bro? You seem a bit out of it," he says.

I start to respond when the short guy with the broad-chest steps onto the terrace and comes directly up to me.

"I don't like how you disrespected my friend," he says with the energy of a man with nothing better to do than argue about women.

"You should tell you friend not to scream at people she doesn't know," I say to the man, feeling my left hand tremble.

Adam looks nervously at us both, but says nothing.

"Listen man, you were the person to violate. You came over and started harassing her."

"Oh is that what she told you?" I ask.

"Me never have to ask her, I saw it," he says, stepping closer with dangerous intent.

I raise my right arm up, palm facing out and he stops moving forward.

"I am an expert in Krav Maga," I say to him, holding his eyes in a grip. "Do you know what that is?"

"I don't give a fuck what it is, just stay away from my girl," he says with a snort.

I do not remove my eyes from him.

"Krav Maga is a martial art dealing with brutally effective self-defense. There is no glamour in a threat, there is only what comes next which means the complete immobilization of your opponent, regardless of his intentions."

"Hey I wasn't threatening yo—"

"The easiest way to disable a person is by destroying their ability to move or rotate a significant limb, by such activities as snapping a wrist, cracking a collarbone or explosively damaging a knee. When a threat is detected and physical confrontation is inevitable, a Krav Maga expert must ask himself, how significant is this threat and is immobilization of the target necessary?"

The guy stands there, watching my hands warily.

"Should I break an arm, disable a leg or simply walk away and avoid the confrontation? However, should the threat be *significant* then the possibly of a mortal injury being afflicted on either party escalates greatly, which means that lethal force might be necessary to end the confrontation."

"What do you mea—"

"Standing where you are relative to the immediacy of our proximity, you could be in possession of a blunt instrument, firearm or something otherwise fashioned to inflict significant injury upon my person which again based on the nature of your approach; threatening, aggressive and predatory makes me have to seriously think of how best to diffuse the situation."

"What if I had a gun, eh? What then?" the man says with a smirk.

"A man with a gun often believes he is not responsible for the idea of a threat when in fact the ownership of a gun forces a person to be even more acutely aware of their responsibility for death."

"Death?"

"If you are in possession of a firearm, you might believe that a man like myself would not also be in possession of one, or in possession of my aforementioned skills. This means that in an outcome involving something as ridiculous and benign as the supposed affectations I have for a girl I do not know or care about would end violently and most likely with your death as well, all because of some idiotic dick wagging."

I step closer and the man flinches.

"To threaten a man is to want to die yourself. Duels do not exist anymore because they were dumb resolutions to simple ideas. Men have no need to fall because of a misunderstanding. Children should not be fatherless because of sperm competition. Necks and arms do not need to be broken because of what a man thinks. Real duels and deaths are relative to what a man *knows,* and you my friend, know nothing."

Confusion and fear mask the man's face now, and after looking at his feet and shuffling around for a few seconds, he walks away.

"Jesus Christ," Adam says, "That was fucking amazing."

"It was not amazing," I reply. "Because I am not amazing."

I don't give him a chance to reply as I leave the venue and head to the car, shaking with anger, not before seeing Brittany walk past me with a young Asian guy, his face calm and unaffected, her hand perched on her ear, clasping her new phone.

Chapter Six

My hands are still trembling as I drive onto the campus of the University of the West Indies the next day. I park and walk across the verdant plains towards the English department to attend my Film Studies class. I sit in the noisy rabble of first year students, mostly girls with no real world experience, faces plastered with the bright smiles that come from the hopeful expectation of an uncertain future with a sprinkling of young men in their presence with faces not yet dark with the shadow that comes from shaving beards daily. I am in the back, away from everyone with my hat pulled low over my eyes, not hearing anything happening around me. Just before the class I took some Xanax and had two drinks but my hands are still shaking and I can't figure why, so I hand in my essay on Bruce Wayne and leave the class twenty minutes before it's over, walk down Ring Road and near the aqueducts, leaning on the old structure, the sun looking beautiful in the sky but I can only define it as beautiful, not see its beauty then I realize I am still trembling and feeling cold and fear begins to grip me. The sky is a stark, cloudless blue but the cloud I know too well is returning. The dull hum has grown into a pulsing monster, augmented by this slight, ever present chill that Kingston has, even in the bright of the daytime. I feel its tendrils touching me everywhere, piggybacking sparks of emotion that increase my emptiness. Isolation floods my brain, despite being in the presence of thousands of students. Many walk past, laughing about nothing, with their young, clean faces, JanSport knapsacks and Adidas sneakers. There is no reality here, no time and no consequence. My stomach is in a tight knot, and in a quick rush, everything gets flat. I see nothing in the green leaves around me and the bright blue sky. I feel nothing when a tall, lithe young woman strolls past, her body screaming to be violated. I overhear an extremely funny joke a young man makes fifty feet away from me, his voice high and clear. His group erupts into laughter, slapping tree trunks and banging on trashcans with the fury of their cachinnation, but I do not laugh. In my eyes I see the cloud emerge from everywhere, a low-rising, quiet mist that leaves footprints behind me as I walk through it. My heart is racing and my hands are shaking even more and I run to the parking lot and sit in the car, close my eyes and turn on the air conditioning, barely feeling the frigid air burning my nose. I want to cough, eat and throw up at the same time as my stomach churns and thrashes. I open my mouth to scream but only a slow, mournful groan comes out. A quick, fleeting memory of my father and mother comes to mind and the tiny hands in my mind reach after the memory, unable to grasp the image of them and myself, somewhere I can't remember. It fades in a flicker into the endless blackness. I grit my teeth and squirm in my seat, trying to breathe normally. The radio screams nonsense to me as I turn it on and I can see the cloud rising higher, brushing the ankles of people walking around, unaware of its presence. I turn on the engine and race over speed bumps and drive off the campus, roaring down Hope Road, but only for a moment, as Hope Road is filled with traffic. I am stuck in my iron box with all the people around me, people staring forward blankly, some wiping sweat from their brows, a man incessantly honking his horn despite the reality that a horn alone cannot move hundreds of cars forward. I make a drink from my cooler in the car but I cannot taste the rum on my lips. I see the cloud in front of me, swishing around the car doors in a thick white blanket, stretching into the horizon. I pull off to a side road and drive towards downtown to escape the gridlock. Before I can think about the people I have seen on the side of the road or the traffic lights that change as I drive through them, before I can take note of the street vendors standing in a thick clump at crossroads and take notice of the people in groups waiting for buses as their voices become a collective human amalgam of unintelligible din, with only a word escaping here and there to make sense of the chaos of our language, before I can stop shaking and get out of the car and just walk, run or scream and try to ignore this rising mist, this fear and panic that nothing will ever meaning anything, before this happens I am in the parking lot of the Carib theatre, the car doors closed and my legs pumping furiously with my long, heavy strides as I pay for a ticket to watch a movie, any movie, and I am sitting down in the almost comfortable, almost accepting darkness of the theater, a theater currently empty. There is no mist in here, just the low *sshhh* that one hears in a quiet space if one listens to very carefully, and I breathe normally for one second, my hands still shaking. But it is only a second, because as the movie trailers start with their loud fanfare and pizzazz, I am constantly startled by the Hollywood booms and heavy sound effects blended in with the noise in front of me as the movie screen flashes rapid cuts of professional video edits displaying men with handsome faces worrying about damsels in distress. I lurch in my seat, leaning forward with my hands over my ears. It is overwhelming this noise, and even in the darkness I can see the mist leaking in by the exit sign, the nothingness spinning around my pant legs. With my left hand I wave some of it away, refusing to accept this dissolution and I leave the theater as the movie starts, stumbling awkwardly back into the light of day.

I cannot stop trembling and I cannot stop hearing everything around me. Outside car horns bellow and grumble, the *pack pack pack* of women's slippers and shoes hitting the ground scream in my ears and everything, everything is happening at once. I am nowhere near this noise, but it is amplified tenfold, and I see the mist is now waist height and I choke with the fear of what it will do to me. I drift through it and to the car, turning on the cold air once more and blasting the radio, giving me slight relief but it is not enough as I drive down to the waterfront and up Marcus Garvey drive, down Spanish town road and then up through Duhaney Park and squeeze through a side road that bisects Manor Park, do some tricky driving around Norbrook and then take the road that leads to where I live, in the hills overlooking Kingston. The navigation occupies me. The roads and their corners, the delicate changes in scenery from highway to byway, the images of undulating asphalt rising into the distant view of green hills and mountains. The cars of various colours around me driving at different speeds. This is the only thing I can be distracted by in finding my way home, my heart still racing and pounding, as I feel choked and see the cloud covering Kingston, rising ever higher. I pull into my driveway and go inside on the balcony seeing nothing but white in my vision; Kingston is gone.

I take a shot of Patrón, kick some Balenciaga shoes out of my way, turn over my two giant red hop sofas and scream at nothing. I take a vase and throw it into the television, barely hearing the crunch of the massive LCD fracturing into pieces. The mist starts to seep into the house, slowly, as if the world was on fire and all that protects people is a choice to stay indoors. I walk into my closet and reach above a series of carefully folded clothes and pluck a black Bottega Veneta tote from the top shelf and walk back into the den where the huge TV is now the ground, black pieces of the LCD glass everywhere, and pull out several vials of coke. I take a hit from one and lie down on the floor, closing my eyes as I see the mist start hovering over the ceiling. My phone is poking my thigh uncomfortably and I pull it out. I dial Andrew, my uncle John, Selena, Brittany, Candice, Adam, Lisa, Mary and Cynthia but no one answers. I try Amy's old number but it doesn't work. The mist is all around me now, the dull hum a loud grumble. Everything is becoming white, and I slap my face to come back to reality. The cloud hesitates in its menacing movement towards me and I hit my face again, seeing it pause and retreat some more. I rush to the kitchen and grab one of the sharp knives from a black set I rarely use and turn around, seeing the mist closer, pushing towards me. With a quick, rapid motion, I slice a part of my arm, screaming as my mind bursts with the reality of the pain I'm feeling. The mist rears up as if hurt itself, and darts out of the kitchen and the living room, retreating quickly back outside. I drop the knife and clutch my arm, dripping blood and run to the balcony seeing the mist pulling away from Kingston, spiraling into a funnel somewhere by the sea, eventually going back into the sky. My screams occupy the house as I run water on my cut and then douse it with alcohol. The pain is all I can feel, shifting my sensation of complete blankness into an acute awareness that I am alive. I douse the cut with alcohol again and scream once more from the pain, buckling, not caring that my diesel jeans are sprinkled with drops of blood. The medicine cabinet has an array of cleaning agents and bandages, and I take some bandages and use masking tape to secure them to my arm. I close my eyes and listen, wondering if the grumble of the dull hum is going to return, but I can't hear it. The fridge is open but I don't remember opening it and I drink some vodka with a few cubes of ice and do one more hit of the co-caine back in the living room, staring at the TV on the floor, looking back at me as if to say *What the fuck dude?* And I sit on the ground, staring at nothing, the Annie Leibovitz book in a corner half-open, everything in disarray and my phone where I left it, still not ringing.

Chapter Seven

I wake up on Wednesday. This is impossible I say to myself, because my Film Studies class is once per week on a Monday. It is unimaginable that I could lose almost two whole days. I'm still in the bloody Diesel pants and the same clothes, my ass sore from sleeping on the floor. The cut on my hand is stained with the slow sleeping of the blood from my self-inflicted wound onto my outer arm. My mouth is painfully dry and I roll to one side, the image of one of the turned over hop sofas in my vision looking as if it is standing right side up. A sudden, insistent cramp hits my stomach and I run to the bathroom to relieve myself. I'm shuddering sitting on the toilet seat as spots of light flash in my vision. Later, after I'm done I get the nagging sensation the mist is going to return, but I don't feel that growing cloud anymore. The flatness of my life has resumed its basic status. I drink some water and take a shower. My stomach growls with the need for food and I walk slowly outside. A deep red is spreading across the sky, signaling the evening. The vista is unapologetically breathtaking, reminding me life in its beauty and pain has no cares or consolations for those who come and go.

I go into the car and flop onto the car seat, today wearing Yayoi Kusama style black and white knee-length shorts, shiny silver oxfords and a Dolce and Gabanna tank top with the image of a screaming gremlin on over eighty percent of the face of the shirt. The evening shifts quickly into the night as I go to a McDonald's and order a large chicken sandwich, large fries, soda and a slice of pie. My mouth feels like a vacuum as I inhale the food which disappears rapidly from in front of me. My phone vibrates and I see that Candice is calling.

"Hello," I croak.

"I saw that you called me," she said.

Ignoring the fact that I called her days before, I respond.

"I'm hungry," I say.

"There is food here," she says.

"I'm coming over," I say, hanging up.

She lives in an apartment complex close to the Sovereign shopping mall. The security guard at the gate gives me a pondering eye as I drive in, parking beside her black Honda CRV. The smell of cement and fresh paint is still in the air, despite construction on the property ending three years before. Her apartment is an attractive split level filled with expensive furniture and interesting glass furnishings. She greets me at the door, wearing nothing but a large Cooyah shirt with the image of a Lion printed on the front. Turning around without hugging me, she goes back towards the kitchen as the smell of food hits my nose and I walk in, closing the door behind me. I have nothing else on my mind except the need to eat; I didn't know hunger could feel like this. Gone is the huge meal from an hour before.

"It's some Chinese food from last night," she says, stirring the food in a pan on a large electric stove.

I barely respond before putting the food on a plate, eating it, two sandwiches and a huge bag of Doritos in her cupboard along with three bottles of her water.

"Wow, someone came here with a monstrous appetite," she says to me, rubbing my stomach as we sit on the sofa in front of her TV, a behemoth larger than the one I'd destroyed at my place.

"What happened to your hand?" she asks, looking at the bandage on my arm.

"Nail scratch," I reply. "I like this TV."

"It's an Aquos," she purrs, pointing a finger at a manual visible through the transparent glass section of her jet black, ultramodern coffee table.

I make a mental note of the TV, even though I have issues with Sharp devices. I flop my feet on the coffee table. I don't feel tired and Candice's hand travels up my thigh and fiddles with the zipper of my shorts. She comments on my Versace boxer briefs as she runs a finger up and down the length of my erect member, but doesn't pull it out, looking at me with an expression that holds a lingering intention.

"Can you do something for me?" she asks, standing up.

"Yes," I reply in a huff, wanting to see her naked, wanting the escape.

She lifts up the shirt and takes it off, her breasts rising with the motion and then falling lightly back into place, sashays past me and towards her bedroom. Returning immediately with her phone in her hand, the hands it to me.

"I want you to choke me while we do it," she says, handing me the phone, which I notice no longer has a broken screen and is already set to the video mode.

She eases me back on the couch, biting the Cooyah shirt on my lap with her teeth and with a flick of her head tosses it to the ground beside us, momentarily sending the scent of fabric softener wafting through the air towards me. My shorts are quickly off and she is still teasing my erect member through the polyester fabric with her tongue and she bites the waistband of my underwear, somehow pulling it off me without using any of her hands. She presses a remote on the table I didn't see before and light house music starts playing from somewhere above us. Holding my cock in her hand, she pauses.

"Are you recording?" she asks.

"Yes," I reply.

She slips it in her mouth, licking and slurping in slow even strokes, with an occasional increase in speed, intermittently looking at the camera. Then she leans back with legs splayed and I enter her, not before taking the Cooyah shirt from the ground, twisting it into a coil and wrapping it around her neck.

Her moans trickle out of her mouth in gurgling sounds as I squeeze the shirt tighter, getting deeper into her as I watch Candice's breasts sway with our movements, her voice echoing throughout the apartment as she touches her clit, fingers slick with a wetness that is already on my thighs. Then I see "CLIFF" come up on screen, and a Swedish House Mafia ring tone plays from the phone and she clamps her thighs around my waist with such strength I am forced to stop thrusting. She answers the phone, with me still inside her. She's on the phone for almost five minutes but I never lose my erection, teasing her non-existent porn star pussy lips, sometimes dipping it in as she speaks, watching her close her eyes and let out inaudible sighs with her mouth, then she comes off the phone and tells me some guy is coming over, but I don't care and I'm raging hard, my back covered in sweat. I take back the phone and start recording again, accidentally dialing some guy named "Daniel" who keeps calling back after I hang up, and I'm watching Candice's face through the sharp screen of her smart phone, she tells me to grab her neck and I do, squeezing it hard, not caring when she coughs because I can feel her vagina tense, more and more, that vagina of hers that is always wet for me and at the ready, then she says *Oh God I'm coming* and buckles against me, still holding the hand choking her neck, and I'm still thrusting as she holds my hand somehow still balancing the camera, and I keep pushing harder, insistent and I feel her come again, her eyes rolling backwards and up, heaving air, not telling me to squeeze less harder and then I come, pulling out and explode on her, over and over in a wet stream, as Candice still shivers in the throes of her second orgasm, shouting *yes, yes, yes* as I tremble and quake, my back muscles tight. I move to the side and she stands up quickly, breasts and body stained with my fluids and walks away from me and towards her room, where I hear her turn on the shower. I sit there for a moment, my Versace briefs still at my ankles, the black and white shorts on the ground beside the coffee table, and my Dolce and Gabbana tank top on the ground as well, though I don't remember taking it off. After putting my clothes back on I head outside, closing the door behind me, the chill of the evening air hitting me on my loins which are still damp, and I sit in the car and pickup the Appleton bottle on the ground of the passenger seat and pour some rum into a cup which was on the ground beside it, relishing the warm mixture. As I drive out I see a man driving into the complex in a black Mitsubishi Pajero, a man who I recognize as the short pale man from the fashion launch at Cube. He is probably charged and ready, unaware that Candice is in the shower washing off my remains. I realize something is wrong with this picture, that something doesn't add up, but all I feel around me is the ever present dull hum of things, hovering and being neither judgmental or repentant, and I forget about the man as I pull out of the complex and head onto the main road.

I get a text from Adam who apologizes for not calling me back recently and he tells me in the message he is having dinner with some friends at marketplace and tells me to come through. After a short drive there, I stroll into the establishment in my sleeveless shirt, walking past a sign that reads, among other things "No sleeveless shirts" and go over to a table where I see Adam and a few people sitting down. The men in the group are almost indistinguishable from Adam, white men with dark hair and low-cropped haircuts wearing a variety of simple Polo shirts. They are with five or so girls, some with mocha coloured skin, two of them white and one dark-skinned girl in a tasteful blue skirt. Adam stands up and gives me a brotherly hug as I wave at everyone sitting at the table. They murmur hello. I sit beside Adam, putting me directly across from the girl with the blue skirt.

She looks at me with the sallow expression that can only come from a lifetime of unusual expectations of men. The kind where she is the center of integral decisions in conversation, movement and form. I don't squirm in my chair as she takes me in, no doubt analyzing me through her highly advanced social filtering system. I turn back to Adam.

"What happened to your hand?" he asks.

"Broken glass," I reply, remarking, "Damn its cold these days."

"Yeah man, I didn't think I'd need to be wearing a sweater in the middle of New Kingston at any point in time," Adam replies.

"You know," came the voice of someone from the table, "They say it's this Global warming thing that's going on."

"Another person replies, "I don't know about all that."

"I think it is somewhat justified," I respond. "All the chlorofluorocarbons in the atmosphere, the increase in demands as our population swells. These things should have an eventual effect on the environment."

The man rubs a hand reflexively on his forehead before answering. "Yes but we might be experiencing a normal pattern in the earth's atmosphere."

"How so?" Adam asks.

"Well, we've only had recorded weather history for about one hundred and eighty years or so, it isn't a stretch of the imagination to think that the earth getting cooler has nothing to do with anything we've done? Maybe it is just a natural process that we are sliding into."

"Like another ice age? Come on," I say.

"Why is that so hard to believe?" the man replies.

"If Anderson Cooper says the world is getting hotter, I believe it," I reply.

A few people at the table chuckle, but the girl across from me is still taking me in with her strange eyes.

"Why do you know Adam?" she asks.

Her probes were reaching out and feeling frantically, trying to penetrate my skull.

"Why do you know him?" I ask.

She lets out what sounds like a grunt and turns to the girl beside her, a frumpy looking girl with pale skin and curly auburn hair. "I love those sandals, are they by Bridget?"

"Yes, I got them yesterday for one twenty," she says.

"You have to tell me where! The pair I'm wearing cost me the usual one fifty," the girl in the blue skirts says.

"Wow you got a good deal," I say to the frumpy girl. "A pair of sandals for one hundred and twenty Jamaica dollars is a good deal."

"The sandals are one hundred and fifty *U.S dollars*," the girl in the blue dress emphasizes, chuckling in unison with her friend, falling back into murmuring with each other. I feign genuine surprise.

Adam takes a bite of his meal and turns to me. "You sure you don't want to eat anything? The food is good."

"No thanks," I say, looking towards his date. "I'm pretty full after this somewhat stimulating conversation."

"At least have a drink," he insists, and I nod in agreement as he pours me a glass of red wine.

"Why do you know Adam?" the girl says again.

"Why do you know Adam, baby?" I say with a song in my voice.

If her face could turn red, it would have. Her shoulders tighten with annoyance. The next words come out cool and cold.

"Don't call me baby, I don't know who you are."

"Adam, why do you know this girl?" I say, turning to him with a smile.

Adam is chewing his food slowly and deliberately, trying not to make eye contact. The rest of the table is blissfully unaware of this strange dialogue, as they murmur in conversation to the backdrop of clinking glass. Finally Adam swallows his food.

"I think we met at Terra Nova was it? We had mutual friends," Adam replies, shooting a worried look at the girl.

"Yes, but *why* do you know her. There must be a deep, underlying reason behind it no?"

"Indie, stop."

"Why should I? She asked a perfectly good question for which I am fastidiously seeking an answer."

I take a gulp of my wine.

"Why does anyone know anyone? I can understand a question like, 'why did you study math' or 'why did you wear that awful dress today' but 'why' someone knows someone else? That goes into the realm of the existential."

"Are you calling me a god?" Adam replies with a laugh, forgetting himself.

"I most certainly am," I reply.

The girl sips her wine slowly, her eyes streaming fire.

"I see you are a semantic joker," she replies.

"No," I say. "To be a semantic joker I'd have to *actually* be talking about semantics. More correctly in this situation I'm a joker of syntax."

"What's the difference?" she replies, raising her eyebrows.

"Oh a world of difference, darling," I say. "To say 'the bourgeoisie are labeled as a classification of a section of society' would be syntactically correct, but to say 'the bourgeoisie are a cut above the rest' relies heavily on the understanding of semantic patterns in common vernacular, but I'm sure you see that."

Her voice came in a growling tremble, "you just love your own voice don't you?"

"No *baby*, I love that you love my voice."

She turns to Adam.

"What the fuck is wrong with your friend?"

She pauses, as if in the throes of anger realizes she made an egregious error, the table now quiet and devoid of the low hum of dull and predictable conversation. She stands up.

"I'm going to the bathroom for a moment."

She storms off, almost hitting a waiter walking with a large tray of steaming food. The people at the table give me an odd, disinterested look, then the murmurs resume at their same decibels. Adam puts his hand on my shoulder and speaks to me in a low whisper.

"What the *fuck* just happened dude? Why do you have an axe to grind with this girl? She's nice."

"Nice people don't ask people why they know their friends."

"Dude, why is that an issue?"

Adams eyes fill with genuine concern and wonder. He doesn't understand any of the jabs that had been subtly thrown, the underlying assessments and assumptions, the war that had just ended with me victorious.

"Forget it man, it's not a big deal. I have to head off anyways."

Looking relieved Adam nods as I said goodbye to the folks at the table, not waiting for a response.

I drive down the road and turn onto Burlington Avenue, seeing a stream of cars in front of me and I remember it is Wednesday and the party Weddy Wednesdays held at the Stone Love headquarters is going on. A man waves me into a parking lot and I pay him two hundred dollars then walk to a man selling jerk chicken and buy half a chicken and start eating the food as I look around me. The fashionistas are all around, men in a rainbow's assortment of pants wearing fake women's Gucci glasses, tight large print shirts, jewelry and colourful shoes. A man strolls by me wearing a leather vest with a yellow merino underneath, sky blue pants and Burberry patterned shoes. With his chest puffed out he makes a beeline for a woman nearby, wearing gold spandex pants and a matching top barely buttoned across the swell of her breasts straining against the fabric. He assumes the position, legs partially open, leaning back with a slight tilt of the neck as he says something to get her attention. She ignores him and walks over to another woman, dressed in platform sneakers and black tights wearing a yellow t-shirt with the image of a hand giving a thumbs up on it, her inhumanly long hair hanging past her shoulders, too luxuriant and too fake under the shine of the amber streetlights overhead. A stream of Japanese girls with perfect thighs and short shorts are walking into the club, with a few guys in tow. Beenie man and ten people are walking towards the venue. He wears a dress jacket with a white dress shirt underneath and slim black pants. His entourage is dressed similarly, and a few of the Japanese girls still outside point at him. He nods at familiar faces in the distance, disappearing into the bowels of the party with his crew. I finish my chicken and bump fists with the cook as I walk towards the venue, the man collecting cash at the door waving me in but I don't know why, and I step in to the party seeing dark rows of people huddled around the sparse layout of trees standing at lonely positions on the property. I go to the bar and a girl with stark blue eyes takes me in as I order a Guinness, gauging my appearance to determine what my vocation might be. Men with locks, braids and heavily patterned hairstyles who look like musicians or are musicians are everywhere, some staring at women with practiced looks of intent, other staring at nothing, as the weed smoke curls upwards into the night from well rolled spliffs in their hands. I walk forward and stand beside a Japanese girl looking intensely forward no doubt trying to lessen the flurry of attention she gets in the Kingston sphere. A few steps in front of me and I am beside a man dressed in full yellow—jeans, pants, shoes and cap—who is dancing mostly by himself, heavy with the smell of carbolic soap and Brut cologne. Dancers jostle for position as the blinding lights of ubiquitous party cameras float around like ghosts and men perform complex routines involving rotations of the hips and knees, twists of the shoulders and synchronized waves of the hands, few sweating despite the demands on their bodies and the thick heat drifting from the center of the crowd. Across from us is Bounty Killer at a table covered in the usual assortment of high end liquor and chasers, his face relaxed as he stands near a wall hidden in the folds of a light entourage. The inner bar is nearby, and I walk there, ordering another Guinness, noticing the huge sign on the wall that lists drinks, but has no prices written for any of them. In attendance are unusually attractive women. Girls with flat, chiseled stomachs and flawlessly unblemished dark skin, full lips and piercing eyes. Some stand in the proximity of famous people, saying nothing at all, in NY caps white v-neck shirts and daisy dukes, the slight movements of their hips like a scream to the senses. Women with an eastern European flair are also sprinkled about, tall physical specimens with long legs, indeterminate ethnicity and cloudy eyes, in the uncertain periphery of artistes who may or may not be sleeping with them. I walk past Beenie man and his entourage, not before nodding at the guy from Connie's fashion show who had worn the gabardine. He is sharp, wearing a black vest over a dress shirt with matching black pants, a Laura B chain belt and Kris Van Assche high top black sneakers. For a moment I am briefly curious about who he is, but I keep walking back to the front of the party, where I see Junior Gong and Julian Marley with a huge set of people under a tree, feet away from the group of Japanese girls, who stand with a relaxed confidence in their group, deliberately away from the crowd. I stand there for a while seeing bodies hover, blur, move forwards and backwards. I process the smiles and the laughs, the dull faces of hard men with hard lives, people searching for status by saying hello to artistes and girls who look bored but have nothing else to do, and the bright eyes of positive men that love their environment. Everything coalesces into a rumbling sensation, then things get slow and I feel like I'm in the middle of an island, with nothing around me. The Stone Love headquarters is gone and I am in the middle of an empty yard with nothing but the trees for company. The music around me starts to dull and fade and I feel frightened, then I'm back in the party, and the sensation of fear keeps crawling up my chest, nothing shifting it, even though I see one of the Japanese girls give me a smile and a nod, but I'm already walking back outside, someone shouts *Artiste!* to me and I don't respond, go back into the car and start driving up Red Hills Road, onto Washington Boulevard, away from the direction of my house, down and far, until I'm on Mandela Highway, the darkness of the night streaking by in a black stream, I drive until I can smell the sea and I'm going towards Hellshire beach, driving into the large housing settlement built by the water. I pull the car onto a lone stretch of sand, staring out at the unfriendly face of the black sea. My feet don't touch the sand because I am still inside, watching the waves roll up and down, up and down the feeling is still choking me and my hands are trembling again. The sea is calling me, its comfort of endless void, its unfeeling, unflinching gaze. I open the glove compartment and take out ten of the Adderall pills. I kick off my shoes and step out of the car, leaving the door open and walk towards the sea, hearing it say *yes, yes, come here my little friend.* The cold water touches my toes and it doesn't sting with cold, just swishes comfortably around my ankles, splashing up a little bit on my shorts. On the beach, I see no one around, though I hear music somewhere in the distance, low and subdued like how I am feeling. My heart is racing in equal levels with the fear I'm experiencing and I raise the hand with the pills to my mouth, then my phone vibrates in my pocket. I curse, thinking I left it in the car, and I pull it out, ANDREW is showing on the phone screen.

"Yes," I answer, my eyes working to make sense of the horizon in front of me.

"Boss, we need to talk," he says with enviable cheer in his voice.

"Now isn't the best time," I say.

"No we do, remember the party is tomorrow and we haven't planned anything yet."

I freeze, remembering the last minute *Inside* party plan. Temporarily, my mind goes back to the concerned face of my uncle, his lips moving inaudibly as the memory of our lunch also brings back memories of my father.

"Are you there?" Andrew says.

I toss the pills into the water, watching them dissolve instantly in the murk.

"Yes," I say breathing out heavily. "I'm still here."

Chapter Eight

Men carry the new Sharp Aquos television from a truck parked in the driveway towards me. I gesture for them to follow me through the driveway past the Range Rover and upstairs towards the living room. There is a need for help with this television because it is seventy inches in size. Chatting amongst themselves as they install the television, the men barely speak to me as I stand and watch the TV rise into the heavens from the new TV stand I bought to accompany it. My phone rings as they pull cables from the Styrofoam packaging.

"Have you called the wholesale store yet?" comes the voice of Andrew.

"Not yet, still getting some things done here," I say, looking at my reflection in the screen.

"Okay well I'm getting a lot of interesting buzz about the party," he replies.

I hear papers shuffling in the background.

"Buzz like what?"

"Well the state of Kingston right now is pretty dreadful and people are hungry for something, anything new to do, so all the people I've contacted seem more than interested."

"Does this mean we need more liquor?"

"Possibly, and we'll probably need some higher end liquor."

"That's not how we usually do it," I say, pointing towards my left when one of the men asks me where the bathroom is.

"Well you don't want these artistes and celebrities showing up and you don't have the kind of liquor they would need."

"It is a free party no?"

"Yes, but we can always have premium liquor on sale."

"That might look a bit tacky," I say with a sigh, sitting on one of the hop sofas.

"How so? People showing up to a person's house and drinking free liquor is tacky enough no?"

"I guess you are right, so what are you thinking?"

"Well the celebs will need liquor for their idiot groupies so, I'm thinking we get a few bottles of Café Patrón, Hennessy and Apple Vodka."

"Apple Vodka? That would be a disgrace."

"Girls like it Indie," Andrew says.

"Fine, Apple Vodka, what about the DJ?" I ask, noticing the color of one of the delivery men's underwear, pink, showing clearly above the waist of his pants.

"The Renaissance guys are out because they were booked, and most already have commitments."

"On a Thursday? What the hell?"

"It's not problem, I have a guy."

"Is he one of those Zip FM people?"

"Please, did you really ask me that?"

"I had to. They are a bit too over exposed. We need people to feel that *Inside* isn't just a cool invite-only party, but a predictor of future talent, or something that represents a mainstay of cool that *we* decide."

"You say this every time Indie. Like I said, I have a guy."

"He better be good," I say, gesturing at no one.

"The dude is one of those DJs that is always playing at Gravity, a good up and comer."

"Cool," I reply.

My phone vibrates and I see that Ed is calling on the other line.

"Update me in a little while, I have to take this," I say, switching lines.

"Ed what's good?" I ask.

"Bossman, you are having an *Inside* party and no one told me?"

"I can't believe the great Ed Walker did not notice this under his all-seeing eye," I remark.

I hear him grunt and breath out heavily, which doesn't signify anger or annoyance, but excitement.

"Well once I heard about it I invited mad bitches to the party," Ed says.

Wind chimes echo in the background of wherever Ed is.

"That sounds great," I say, "These 'bitches' are DTF of course?"

"Do you even have to ask Indie?"

"We need people to have crazy, epic stories. People need to dream about what happens here tonight. Fantasize, spread the word, be intrigued, alarmed and disappointed they weren't on the list. We need to engender it all."

Ed laughs.

"Okay mister public relations. Also, I'm gonna bring a few bottles of Reserve for the team," Ed says, now sounding busy.

"Bring some Café Patrón and Apple Vodka," I say to him.

"Egad Indie, sounds like you have a bitch rolling you want to get drunk."

"No," I say with a laugh.

"It's done," Ed says, hanging up before I say goodbye.

The men finish with the television and walk back outside to the delivery truck. I watch it drive down the hill and around a bend shrouded in the thick shadow of an outcropping of trees, when my phone rings again.

"Connie," I say.

"Indie I heard about the party, I have a few friends from out of town coming and they are leaving on Saturday, can they come?"

"Yes, but I hope these aren't the same friends from Alberta," I say.

"Just one," she replies.

"Is it Eric?"

"Yes," she replies.

"Connie the man is a bit... unhinged. He can come, only if you keep the little animal on a leash."

"No problem," she says.

I put down the phone for a second, walking back into the living room and stare at the television. The device returns my pondering look in a shout of silence. Turning it on, I squint briefly from the glare. Music pounds from the built-in speakers and I feel a slight rush as images flash on screen, crystal clear and super sharp. The television that I destroyed previously was thirty-seven inches in size, more than enough for a life of little use, but this one, this felt like it needed a sound system and accessories, an endless array of channels and subscriptions that would take advantage of its high definition features. This TV held the promise of nights with friends grouped around its lambent screen laughing and pointing at whatever comedy we were watching play out, as we drank rum and ate Nacho chips, the night just being ours. I saw a girl beside me, cuddled up and warm after a night out, the silk sheets slipping off us as the romantic comedy or whatever token movie becomes obvious as not being the real center of attention, my lips would find hers and the TV would watch everything that happens next, silently. My phone rings again.

"Yes sir, how's it going?" came a voice I wasn't familiar with.

"It goes," I reply.

"The party tonight is going to be epic!" the man says.

Whoever he is, there is a remarkable passion in his voice, something magnetic and attractive.

"Hopefully. To whom am I speaking?" I ask.

"Chris, man, this is Chris, you don't remember me?"

"Actually no," I reply.

"We've met before, at the Cube Fashion party and I saw you at Weddy Wednesdays the other night, you looked a bit out of it," he says, his voice rippling with genuine concern.

My mind flashes to the night before, the darkness of the beach swelling in front of me, hopelessness choking my neck with thick, invisible chains. I think of Weddy Wednesdays and think that I spoke to no one, only nodding at the fellow in the sharp outfit. I realize who it is. The man who was wearing the gabardine at the fashion show, and the high-end clothes. He was resourceful. Getting my number wasn't easy.

"Cool. What do you need Chris?" I ask.

"Just checking to see if I'm on the list for later," he says with a smile in his voice.

"Done. I'll add you plus two," I say.

There is a pause on the line.

"I usually roll with my dogs but tonight I think I might entertain a special lady, you know how it is," he says, the smile in his voice reaching uncomfortably through the phone speakers and rubbing my arm.

"Yes I do, you plus three. I have to go now, respect Chris."

After calling the providers for liquor in the evening and shooting out a text message to a caterer that would provide "limited finger food" as displayed in our e-mail blast, I step outside the living room, away from the balcony and exit the house at the back. The yard is a vast gap of space behind the house, untidy and half-groomed. Fat mango trees with low hanging branches stand in a group near a dust-covered Jacuzzi. I pull out a lawn chair from a set of three behind a storage shed, ignore the grumble of hunger in my stomach and sit on it, looking up at the painfully blue sky above me. My hand falls to the side of the chair, flopping on the cool grass, which tickles the hairs on my forearm.

"Inside, Inside," I say to no one.

As I lie there, I think. The original party had just been a fragment of an idea, something that popped up out of nowhere one night, as Andrew and I had hung outside a jerk chicken spot, chewing the spicy meat and talking under the warm night air. There needs to be a cool private party, Andrew had said to me, and I had nodded, agreeing that constantly going to clubs and lounges was getting boring. I said it would need to be under the radar, something only insiders would know, and thus the name *Inside* came to be. Originally we called it *Inside: Kingston* but it was too much to explain to people, many of whom thought it was a documentary launch or the name for some kind of photo book. Planning the party hadn't been difficult at all. People like the lure of anything free; free clothes, free liquor, free punani. Our first event had ten people, all guys, young and horny, getting wasted on Appleton rum that all eventually ended up at a strip club in New Kingston. Some guy who got a blowjob from a Ukrainian stripper that night had been the most vocal advocate of the party, word of which went through the Kingston Chinese telephone and became a story where the first party some how involved free alcohol and an ensuing orgy with ten Ukrainian strippers. Regardless of how this was obviously not true, the second one we held had significantly more people, mostly guys, but a few curious girls as well. Andrew's house was the perfect venue. It had a palace-sized gate, swimming pools and a party deck that could accommodate dozens of people, plus a long flat stretch of road outside for easy parking. The celebrity thing happened pretty organically. Once we made the party invite only and got a few sponsors on board through some cousin of Andrew's who worked for Appleton, people were clamoring to get on the guest list, which we limited to one hundred people with the exception of celebrities who generally got in without any hassle. Before the incident where a drunk businessman pulled out his gun on a teenager at the party who was in a group of people connected with some shady fellows, it was the ultimate popup party. This was all done without any press, just word of mouth. It ended shortly before my parents boat accident, and I remember what I liked was the structure of it all. The people calling to be listed, setting up the venue, ordering the drinks and handling the various kinds of people that came in, trying to project what I called the "event fallout", essentially if we'd get high ratings or low ratings and seeing which current hot artiste or celeb would come the party without being invited by us. It had been fun, and as I lay there, I wondered if this would be my last one.

* * * *

Cars drive past the entrance of Andrew's house at about eleven. The party is slated to start at nine p.m, which means by twelve everyone will start arriving. The setup contains a series of long, slightly curved plastic tables on either side of the main patios, where the pool is covered. The speakers and DJ setup are also by the pool, where DJ Yaya, dressed in a sleeveless shirt showing ridiculous musculature stands with his headphones on, intently focused on his equipment. Behind him, stretching up into the air are two large Appleton Rum banners, billowing slightly in the night breeze. Not much else is obvious in this setup; the house is more than enough in itself to project a sense of lifestyle and pomp. The pool has marble accents around its perimeter, the party deck is outlined by intermittent sets of thin oak fences and tall, thick plants tastefully hover at its boundaries, giving the flatness of the deck a verdant touch. The house, palatial and rising upwards into the darkness bubbles with a dark, exciting energy. All those empty rooms, all these warm bodies. A friend of Andrew's, a guy named Beckford, is manning the list, even though his eyes are already red from alcohol consumption. I'm parked outside near the front gate, since Andrew's garage is already filled with his family cars; his custom Honda Civic, father's Toyota Prado, mother's E-Class Benz and an old Suzuki Vitara that serves as a backup vehicle. They are absent, on a sojourn to Miami for a week. He walks out of the house, on the phone, in a dark blue Paul Smith blazer, undershirt and dark pants. After he sees me and waves hello, I walk to the poolside, hail the DJ who immediately says "Wanna big up Indie in the building!" Smirking, but not because of the DJs wit, I walk away and check with one of the waiting staff (there are six working tonight, three at each bar) if the premium liquor was ready. One of the men, a short man with a pleasant face who introduced himself as William took me inside into Andrew's parent's study, where I saw endless boxes of Patrón, Hennessy and Moet. The regular Appleton rum and Vodka would be at the bar for invited patrons. Nodding to myself, I walk outside, seeing a slow trickle of people walk in. I notice Connie and a few of her friends coming in, including her friend Eric, who is already walking with the gait of someone who has been drinking considerable amounts of liquor. *Leash,* I mouth to Connie as I walk back inside, looking on the list for no reason, nodding at Beckford, then stand by the leftmost bar where I can see people slowly filling up the pool area, standing relaxed with drinks in their hand, the backdrop of Kingston behind them.

It doesn't take long for the noise of dozens of cars pulling up and people clamoring to get in begins. Women dressed in elegant skirts and pantsuits, guys in sports jackets, cool dress shirts and designer pants. As I usually do, I watch the procession of people enter the party, analyzing personalities based on what they are wearing, noting to my self if they stand alone or by the DJ and how quickly they consume alcohol. Andrew comes over to me, with a bottle of Appleton Reserve in one hand, a drink cup in the other.

"Let's make reggae music, get famous and have sex with miss Jamaica candidates," Andrew says, spilling some of his drink.

"You can have sex with them, I'll make babies with one or two and forever be enshrined in the hallways of men with a sign that reads: *HAS MADE A BABY WITH A MISS JAMAICA.*"

A brief seriousness falls over Andrew's face and he stands straight for a moment.

"Someone, no *somebody* should be notorious for fooling around with the runner ups," he says to me.

"No one cares about a miss Jamaica runner up. Do you remember who the runner up for the first ever American Idol TV show was?"

"Kelly Clarkson," Andrew says with a smile.

"Nice try, but I know you know that she won the whole thing! In the same vein, what's the point in becoming a super famous artiste if you are the guy that slept with some Miss Jamaica runner up?"

"They are still hot," he argues, pouring more Appleton reserve into his cup, not adding any chaser.

"Hotness alone doesn't fit into the delicate paradigm of the elite Jamaican socialite status quo. People want a miss Jamaica, because people will say, Do you know so and so person is dating a miss Jamaica? People will reply, really? He is? He must be of some merit. And the beat goes on and on."

The thin, early crowd gives scattered shouts of approval as the DJ plays Half Pint's "Greetings" and Andrew slaps a hand on my shoulder.

"Holy shit! I *have* slept with a miss Jamaica," he says with eyes open.

I laugh and fold my arms, cocking my head while throwing him a dubious squint.

"Was this pre or post victory?"

"Pre."

"Then it doesn't count," I reply.

"Ah, dammit, why?"

"The girl you slept with two years ago who becomes a miss Jamaica isn't the same person. Both her persona and her holiest of holies evolve at the same time."

"Hah! I disagree, the person is the same," Andrew says, poking me in my chest.

Waving my hands I say, "The person is the same, but what evolves is the idea of them. What you did not sleep with, was the idea of who they would become. Does it matter if you were the guy who slept with Halle Berry or Angelina Jolie before they became world famous? What matters is the dude that has her naked and wet for him after she hits the big time. Let me ask you, did you sleep with this miss Jamaica chick *after* she took the title?"

"No," Andrew says in laugh. "She was dating some big party promoter."

"That my friend, is what we call the evolution of vagina," I say.

Andrew laughs and walks briefly over to a set of people coming in, Gregory the bank executive, and a few fellows that look like his brothers. He escorts them to the bar and pours them all drinks mixed from his bottle. Then I see Ed at the gate, in a black Prada jacket with a striped undershirt. He gives me his usual smile of power, pointing at the girl beside him, who is the same young woman from the Cube Fashion party. A server asks me something about ice, and I point him towards the kitchen and when I turn back around, I see Amy again but she is walking beside Beckford, not being checked for being on the list because of whom she is with. She is with Kwame Anthony, one of Jamaica's most famous musicians.

"Hi," she says to me, not shaking my hand. "Do you know Kwame?"

"Who doesn't?" I say with a smile.

"Respect," Kwame says to me, shaking my hand in a firm grip.

Kwame Anthony came from one of those families that everyone knew about, the kind where the father was a famous Lawyer from an equally famous legacy of lawyers, the kind of man who defended Jamaica's worst and was always in the paper, a man notorious for enjoying life as much as he worked to protect it. This influence no doubt affected the young Kwame, who decided to grow his hair in locks at Campion College, where it was not allowed, and he was promptly expelled, despite the protestations of his well-connected father.

The story goes that his disillusion with this reality of acute prejudice created a rift between certain ideologies his father held and he left home, moving from a comfortable Jack's Hill residence to somewhere off Hagley Park road, where he spent time selling fruit in the street, working in a wholesale shop and redefining his sense of Jamaica through the eyes of days under hot sun and nights in hot rooms. His first musical hit, "Street Walker", was a ballad about this time, detailing the time period when he as a teenager went out into the world alone and how learning about the true Jamaica forced him to do music. His clear voice was filled with range, and the sound systems from all parts played his songs with gusto, as his music hit the radio waves locally and abroad without Kwame spending any money on payola.

His look was a delicate blend of his father and mother. From his father, he received the height and dominating presence that worked well in a courtroom, from his mother certain delicate features that gave his face a relaxed soulfulness, perfect for music videos and television, perfect for the emotive reggae music that captured the heart of millions. Eventually there were whispers of a record deal with Universal records or Island records, whispers of a tour in Europe where the world had been waiting on him to go because he refused to travel without his original band members from Hagley park road, whispers of millions of U.S dollars waiting for him, officially breaking him away from his family's legacy.

The album came, *My Revelation,* and it took the world by storm. On it, was an image of him shot on a lone beach, running with a coconut in his hand, shirtless and smiling in white pants, his then shoulder length locks swaying in a breeze no one could feel but only imagine, the photographer creating the ultimate image of his marketable look, a man from Jamaica with a voice from the heavens.

Fame gave him tours to Europe and collaborations with groups like UB40 and the Rolling Stones. Often he appeared on David Letterman to promote a new single, one of his tracks "Sensimilla Warrior" played endlessly in a Quentin Tarantino art house film and briefly, his music was featured in an Apple Campaign for a sporty new colorful line of iPods, saying his "warm music fits the vibe of the world's best music player in your hand".

He dated some of the islands hottest women, from miss Jamaicas to other female artistes of repute, was linked to supermodels in Paris and some rumors said Gwyneth Paltrow, which was never confirmed, all the while putting out three albums, *The Trial, Love is Dark* and *Real Real Love* which all went multiplatinum, further solidifying his base as one of the world's most renowned artistes. Women kept his pictures on their phones, taped photos on their walls of images of him from a special photo shoot of him organized by the Jamaica Observer, cawed at him at concerts and professed undying love. All he would do is give a smirk and a soft laugh, telling everyone all he had was love for them, looking downwards and to the right as he said this, a personality tick people loved. They said he was the next Bob, the next artiste to really take Jamaica to the next level, a man with such a groundswell of talent, personality and success he roamed freely without any hassle, despite his obvious wealth. Kwame Anthony, the living legend, standing in front of me with Amy by his side.

"Good party going on you know," he says to me, effortlessly ensnaring me with his eyes.

"I—I'm glad you are enjoying yourself," I reply.

"Kwame doesn't drink so we were wondering if you had any coconut juice or anything like that inside here," Amy says to me, her eyes flooded with contentment.

My next reply comes out in a stutter.

"Coconut water? Yes, I think we have some."

My left arm is trailing against the kitchen wall, fingers scratching the undulating lumps of white paint done in that style on purpose, ears tickling with the throbbing of bass from the speakers outside at my current position as I walk through the hallway of high ceilings towards Andrew's industrial sized refrigerator, open it and take out a large bottle of Coconut water, noticing it is not a local brand and go back to Amy and Kwame Anthony. They are in the hallway I just walked through, admiring a painting on the wall I did not see before. The difference between their body language is vast in my mind. Kwame Anthony has a level of relaxation that comes simply from being who he is. Everything, his chuckles and manner-isms are his to command. Everyone likes him for who he *actu-ally is*. Amy, though trying her best, is in uptown groupie mode. She's standing a little too closely, agreeing a little too quickly with what he says, but still seems reasonably balanced in the presence of such a megastar. Her fashion ensemble, black leggings and a long sleeved lace top showing all her bodily perfection isn't a bad move either. For a moment, I think I see

Kwame Anthony give her what appears to be a lingering stare, but it is nothing more than a brief flash of his eyes at hers. These situations seem to have man pitted against woman, beauty versus experienced conquistador, but it is never true. Status is the most addictive drug in Kingston, and no woman can resist it. Though it may seem Amy has control, she has none. Kwame Anthony could be on a flight to Spain, Italy or Dubai tomorrow and have a thousand Amys ready and waiting for him. But she knows this, and for that reason, she is already lost. She touches his shoulder as they speak, gesturing at something. I cough to interrupt their reverie.

"Here's the Coconut water," I say, handing it to Kwame.

A look of sheer appreciation comes over his face, so genuine and so full of life I find my chest filling with warmth.

"Respect and so many thanks," he says to me, bowing his head slightly then turning around.

"We'll get cups outside," Amy says to me, eyes looking forward, away from me, her hand still on his shoulder as they walk in tandem back into the fray of the party outside.

A trembling starts inside me on a low frequency. I reach into my pockets for something to calm down with, but I left all my drugs in the car. Stepping quickly outside into the throng and nodding at Wayne Marshall who is hanging with Baby Cham and Sean Paul, I am stopped by a firm hand on my shoulder. It is Andrew, he looks concerned.

"We need another table," he says.

"Another table? Why?"

"Because Usain Bolt is walking in," he says, pointing with his nose.

Bolt and a few tall guys walk in, flanked by Christopher Martin and a few more guys. Reasonably famous celebrities around him seem dull as he walks past, leaving a hint of excitement in his wake.

"Ah, okay," I say.

There is always a logical need for a table with certain guests, but there are already seven tables dotted at various points in the venue. I rustle up a few of the waiting staff and we go quickly inside Andrew's house, walking behind him, past the kitchen and into the living room. Antique furniture is everywhere, and Andrew says 'no' to quite a few objects resembling tables before we see an old chest of drawers that had been converted into a high desk. Incidentally it is white, matching the curved tables outside.

"Perfect," he says.

The guys lift the table carefully, up and over a marble statue of a naked woman frozen in the throes of ecstasy, past porcelain figurines mysteriously loitering on a platform adjacent to where the table was, and through the living room, which is a maze of high end furniture and rugs, then go outside, where the Bolt camp has already found a good spot, facing the pool near one of the palm trees. The table and a cloth are setup quickly. The group orders several bottles of all the high-end stuff we have. I don't say anything to Bolt or his group and walk to the kitchen, telling one of the guards to make sure people don't go upstairs unless they have Andrew's consent, to which he nods, smiling, obviously excited to be at this event, while I walk to the fridge, slowly, deliberately, pulling a bottle of water from the freezer. I sip on it.

I hear feet coming down the stairs beside the kitchen. Eric, the man from Alberta drifts over to me, body thick with the scent of alcohol. He pats me heavily on the shoulder, sending waves of annoyance through me.

"Sean Paul is cool man," he says in a sleepy voice. "He gave me a shot of Patrón."

"Where is Connie?" I ask, my face a blank slate.

Eric smiles and walks away from me, towards a set of attractive young women with expectant faces at the end of the hallway. There are people coming in, people that weren't on the list, and I make a mental note to tell the security guards that letting in someone simply because they are white isn't the policy of *Inside,* that if you aren't allowed in, you can't come in, and I'd possibly go into a spiel about post-colonial hegemonic ideology, but then Connie comes into the kitchen, pulls me to one side and asks me where is the weed, because 'people' want to smoke and I go try to find Andrew who has disappeared and run into Ed in the kitchen, who has a dealer, and a text or two later has a solution.

"He'll be here in thirty minutes," Ed says with a smirk, his face dotted with beads of sweat.

I thank Ed and go back outside, receiving hellos from a few faceless girls I see all the time that now know this is my party, shake hands with a fellow from high school and then Tristan, who is dressed uncharacteristically sharp in a white dress shirt with a thin black tie and skinny black jeans, then run into Chris who had called me earlier, who is flanked by a few hard-faced men with practiced body language dripping in high fashion clothing. Today he is wearing red leather pants, a thin fitting Gucci shirt with the same Balenciaga tote attached to his waist. Get drinks, I say to them, before walking near the front, where Beckford is trying to deal with more unlisted people that want to get in. I hear *Indie! Indie!* A few times from people outside and ignore the name calls, watching Amy laugh with Kwame Anthony, who gets a bear hug from Usain Bolt as they talk about something enviously interesting. A sigh escapes my mouth and I walk back to the kitchen, drink some more water and a guard hands me a huge Samsung phone, telling me that a girl dropped it but refused to take it back from him. As weird as this sounded, I nodded, took the phone to the DJ, who announced that it was missing, standing amongst a thick throng of people now, carefully orbiting the pool, including Candice, in a breathtaking deep cut black dress showing her perfect breasts, face quiet as she stands beside a man, different from the guy I saw last time, a short older white man with a comfortable smile plastered on his face. Back by the bar, I see Eric talking to Valerie, who shoots me a weird look. Tonight

Valerie looks much younger, her olive skin glowing in the nighttime.

"I didn't know you threw parties," Valerie says to me.

"Hey baby, we were talking here," Eric interrupts, standing uncomfortably close.

"I don't throw parties," I reply, making a crocodile smile, walking away quickly, not liking Eric's constant, wobbly stare at me.

A flurry of activity is happening at the gate, and Andrew has reappeared and we walk over, seeing a bunch of people loitering outside. Beckford looks at me nervously as he holds the list, dots of sweats on his forehead. Outside, I see Bounty Killer with an entourage of five, Flame and an entourage of no less than twelve people including Cynthia, and a stream of hangers on, some of whom who see me and start shouting my name. We let Flame, Bounty and his people in and I ignore a few people that sneak in through the bomb rush for the gate. Andrew chats to Bounty Killer while I avoid Cynthia's gaze, tell the waiting staff that we'll need a few more private tables from somewhere, anywhere, then I head back to the kitchen where I pause, seeing the crazy girl from the Subaru launch party at Gravity. I sigh inwardly as she catches my eye, her eyes a cool brown and devoid of the fire I'd seen in them that night.

"Hey!" she says with friendly gusto. "I remember you!"

"Too well," I say, not moving towards her.

"I'm sorry about the last time I saw you," she says with mild sincerity. "I was drunk."

"And now? What state are you in?"

She emits a sweet laugh, a laugh I immediately dislike.

"I'm sober," she replies.

She lifts her drink towards me. "Well, mostly sober."

I lean on the rippled paint wall.

"You know, if my students ever knew how I reacted that night to you, I'd be in so much trouble," she adds.

"Oh?"

"Yes, an English teacher shouldn't be caught being so *profane*," she says.

My eyes narrow. "You are an English teacher? You should know the answer to this question, English teacher. What is the antithesis of an antecedent?"

She pauses, fingering the ice in her drink.

"You should know that social savvy has nothing to do with the idea of grammatical understanding. Teaching, instruction and peer mentoring is inextricably interwoven with the reality that the person with the reins leads the horse."

"What do you mea—"

"Should a student ask you a particular question, for example the one I have just posed, which I will pose again, that is: 'What is the antithesis of an antecedent' it is only right, no *just* that you as their provider, their gateway to knowledge and future self inference should have an answer to the question."

She shuffles awkwardly in place, and I see the slightest stirring of the fire in the girl's eyes coming back, but I'm already walking out of the kitchen, angry at nothing in particular, feeling sparks of discomfort when I think about Kwame Anthony and Amy, not caring about the crowd making noise for DJ YaYa (who is pretty good) standing by one of the bars, staring at the crowd, seeing the sea of familiar faces and damaged goods, Chris Gayle dancing with his friends near the pool, Andrew dancing erotically with that girl I'd met before, Britney or Brittany, a few people waving at me but not coming over, Eric, drunk and disorderly, in the arms of a dark-skinned woman staring deeply into his eyes. Music roars and the crowd's energy hits a fever pitch, I can smell the rum in the air and see a stream of car lights on the streets as more vehicles pull up to the house. This is the biggest *Inside* we've ever had, and I realize the list will soon be meaningless, liquor might very well run out, and people will have stories for days to come. The realization doesn't affect me, and walking back inside, music trailing behind me, I sit in Andrew's parents living room on a giant black couch with lion's paws for legs. My eyes are squeezed shut, trying to drown out everything around me. I feel the mist returning, the choking pointlessness of everything. I think about the glove compartment of my car outside, all the pills and vials hidden in there, I want them, but I don't move. I focus on the logic of the party, the structure of who is there, the layout of the table, the angle of view from the first bar to the next, the architecture of the pool and understanding designs that involving curvature and depth, standard water chlorination levels and pool cleaning times, but my mind is slowly getting dull, the wisps of white particles drifting slowly towards me, a call to the black void. Then I see Amy dancing with Kwame Anthony in my mind, her body already his, her vagina wet just from his presence, me an increasingly distant memory, and then I get up, needing the pills, needing something dark. For the night so far I haven't had a drink and I don't care, there are drinks in the car where the pills are, all of them, waiting for me, chuckling and giggling with negative promise only too eager to be swallowed. Strolling through the crowd, I don't hear much, nothing except my own footfalls, the subdued beating of my heart and the slight clink my belt makes against itself. Passing the bar, then the pool, I'm near the gate, when a hand touches me. I turn to see a girl with frighteningly piercing eyes. She is tall, dressed in a stylish, slightly oversized grey top that shows a lone, bare shoulder, tight black pants and grey Dr. Martens boots. Her face is attractive in an unnerving way, with strong eyes, high cheekbones and delicate lips that form into a slight, natural smirk, her black hair pulled back into a 1980s style side ponytail.

"I have an answer for your question," she says to me.

The noise of everything around me returns in a thunderclap.

"Question, what question?" I ask, my heart fluttering slightly in the pathway of her eyes.

"A man poses a question, that man must remember the question," she says to me in song, her voice smooth and hypnotic.

"Okay, I remember the question. Wait you were there? In the kitchen?"

"One never knows what lurks in the shadows," she says in the same singsong tone.

Furtively, I raise an eyebrow. "What is your answer?"

"Chuck Norris."

Pausing, my heart still behaving on its own, I look at her again, her face, her lips. She must be an illusion.

"Why would you say that?" I ask.

The girl smirks, holding her drink in her left hand, resting the elbow of that arm on the on the wrist of her right arm, wrapped around her ribs.

"An antithesis tends to be an opposite, and the technical opposite of an antecedent is a postcedent. Since an antecedent gives meaning to the proform which follows it, in a postcedent, meaning is already established before the noun appears. Nothing establishes precedent like Chuck Norris. He is always before, never after, always victorious, never the loser. He was before thought, and always will be before thought, therefore HE not anything else, is the antithesis of an antecedent."

A strange feeling rolls over me in cascading waves, I notice my heart isn't pounding and I no longer need to go to my car. I am smiling.

"Wh-whats your name? I'm Indie," I ask, extending my hand.

She smiles at me, and briefly my heart flutters again.

"Berlin," she says, holding my hand in a firm grip.

The world briefly pauses into a space I can't explain, as behind me the crowd cheers about something that doesn't matter.

Chapter Nine

It is the look she constantly gives me that holds me stead-fastly in place, as the lure of the tablets in my car begin to wane. The ubiquitous dullness around me thinning, drifting somewhere else for the moment, being slid out of my vision by a burgeoning curiosity. The long, slope of her legs, the inde-terminate shape of her torso, hidden by the oversized shirt she wears, and those eyes, brown eyes, sharp and exquisitely con-toured, pulling at me with herculean magnetism. However, truth returns to the fore of my mind, as I stand near a sea of people cheering and drinking, stinking with the promise of passionate encounters, the promise of the night.

"I know a man," I begin. "A man that wants to die."

"A man you say?" Berlin replies, her smirk turning into a smile.

"Yes, A man wants to die."

"A man needs to be an itinerant sex worker."

"Excuse me?"

"A man needs to drift between the grey areas of society and wallow in its dregs, wearing black pumps and glittery briefs to make his day to day ends meet."

I laugh.

"A man needs options," I say, gesturing.

"A man has nothing but his cock and his wits in this life," Berlin replies assertively.

Shrugging my shoulders, I say, "But a man needs real tools."

"A man is born with the only tool he'll ever need. The best tool God gave him, dangling between thigh number one and thigh number two."

"A man may have erectile dysfunction."

Berlin steps forward, I smell a quality, foreign fragrance coming from her.

"A man has an ass and off season Versace biker shorts. A man can survive."

A laugh comes out of me from the depth of ancient memories, memories of marigold skies and candy stained lips, waking up thrilled on Christmas mornings to expectantly open gifts, memories of the long, soft hugs of my mother, hugs before wine bottles became her best friends, before she became quiet and obsessed with work, memories before it all.

"Walk with me," she says, turning around, heading towards the bar nearest the pool.

Drifting lightly to the bar, she smiles with one of the servers, making him blush as she pats his shoulder after requesting our drinks. Then she turns, winks at me, sending more flurries through my chest, picks up two drinks and walks over.

"Thoughtful, " I remark, reaching for the drink.

"These are mine," she says, sipping one.

"Oh," I say, looking at the server, gesturing for a drink.

She thrusts the cup in my hand, spilling some of it on the tips of my fingers.

"Obviously this is for you silly! You need one, wound up as you are."

I taste the drink, grimacing as Apple Vodka hits the roof of my mouth.

"Why am I wound up, pray tell?"

"Any fellow walking around with an oversized wallet is wound up," she replies emphatically, her eyes temporarily occupied with a raunchy display of dancing beside us.

"And a girl dressed in an oversized Merci Beaucoup shirt and Dr. Martens isn't wound up? Isn't trying to send a message? "

She laughs, a laugh that brings the sun out at night.

"You are reaching, Indie. I don't need to send a message, the message is obvious. I am the prize and I know it."

"But if you th—"

"The purpose of a wallet is portability, end of story. A man who walks with a big wallet is either overcompensating for something else, or spent too much time playing in mommy's closet, trying on her high heels when she went to the super-market."

"Standing high on our opinion pedestal are we?" I ask, putting down my drink and replacing it with one the server brings over.

Calm washes over me as the familiar taste of rum swirls in my throat. Berlin reaches into her back pocket and pulls out a large brown wallet almost identical to mine.

"Self-deprecation is sometimes the best form of self-flattery," she says, laughing again.

I am stuck smiling at her, a cube of ice melting in my mouth, my body warm, despite the chilly night air. Opening my mouth to speak, I stop, seeing a girl come over. Her appearance is characteristic of Berlin's, although she is shorter, with blonde hair and blue eyes.

"This is Marga," Berlin says, "She works for a company that handles tours for reggae artistes going to Europe. Marga, this is Indie."

Marga gives me a perfunctory nod and a weak handshake.

"I need you for a moment," she says to Berlin, gesturing with her head towards the direction of any number of celebrity tables.

"A woman is being summoned," Berlin says to me as they walk away, me staring at the sway of her hips and the dark, sun-tanned shine of her lone, bare shoulder. I turn to the bar.

"Another drink please," I say.

There are people everywhere now, so many that several potted plants are a little bent out of shape and the scent of cigarette and weed smoke lightly tints the air. My mind is no-where, thinking about Berlin, and the laugh she brought out of me. Another flash of memory surges to the front of my mind, an image of a park, a park where I'm running in the grass, and someone is behind me, chasing me, a face I can't remember.

"Dude, you won't guess who is here!" comes the voice of An-drew.

He is smiling too broadly, patches of sweat visible on the collar of his Paul Smith shirt, bottle of Appleton Reserve in his hand. He has no cup.

"Who?" I say.

"The miss Jamaica I fucked! She's here!"

Before I can find out who she is, there is distance between us, his legs moving in quick strides away from me as he laughs loudly, bumping fists with three music producers and Beenie Man, who I didn't know had arrived. I walk towards the kitch-en, nodding at the security guard standing nearby. Ed is com-ing from downstairs, his jacket gone, striped shirt looking resplendent.

"Told this dude if he didn't let me piss up stairs it would be his job," Ed says with a smile.

I smile.

"But *bro*, that girl from the other night, the one with the big ass, she is a fucking freak *bro.*"

"Oh?"

"She's been putting my Pilates workouts to the test," Ed says, easing past three people standing near the kitchen sink, opening the refrigerator. He takes out a slab of cheese, breaks off a chunk and bites into it, leaving the cheese on the counter and the fridge door ajar.

"What do you mean?" I ask, putting the cheese back into the fridge, closing the door.

"Pilates builds core, and when you get your core strong *bro*, you can fuck forever. But this chick, BRO! She's a racehorse in the bedroom. The first night I broke my television going at it with her."

"Broke your television?"

He pats me on the shoulder several times rapidly. "We fucked in the car before coming into the party, I'm so turned up right now!"

"Where is she now?" I ask.

"I dunno, talking to Sean Paul or some junk," Ed says.

He strolls out in a wave of energy, and I follow him outside into the throng. There is barely any space around the edges of the pool now, and the party deck is packed. I glimpse Berlin and Marta somewhere near Bolt's table, but they step into the crowd and are swallowed by the bodies.

"Indie!" a voice says.

It is Adam, in a dark purple suit, with the girl from marketplace, who'd been in the blue dress, who tonight is wearing a black top, salmon coloured ruffle skirt and black high heels. I give him a quick hug and nod at the girl, who gives me an indifferent nod in reply.

"This is his party," Adam says to me.

The girl's eyes look at me with slightly enhanced interest.

"Is this your house?" she asks.

"Every house is my house," I reply with a smile. "Get some drinks guys!"

I pat Adam on the back and walk towards the pool, spotting the intern from Condé Nast with Jenna the dancer, and Connie. They are all dancing with men in the same position, asses to the sky, leaning forward. The intern spins around when Vybz Kartel's "Dumper Truck" starts playing, now grinding the guys hips. Jenna is being pecked on the neck by the fellow she's with, and Connie seems lost in liquor and the moment with her guy. I ease past them, carefully. The DJ spots me.

"YOOOOOOO! Pull up!" he says

The music stops.

"We just wanna big up men like Indie and Andrew, the Inside crew! If you are feeling this party I want everybody to say BOMBOCLAAT!"

The crowd roars *BOMBOCLAAT* in unison, then the DJ immediately drops Popcaan's "Party Shot" and bodies start moving dangerously fast around me, people patting me on the shoulder and hugging me, someone gives me a toxically strong drink, a bombshell girl standing in a group of three nearby me suddenly runs over, shoving her ass on my groin, moving with expert rhythm to the song, then I see Chris smiling and holding a bottle of Hennessy in his hands, laughing as he gives me a nod of approval. Soon I break away from the girl, ducking as Chris Gayle looms over me, dancing with some of his friends, then two girls run past me with only their bras showing, towards the pool. It is then I really notice the pool cover is gone, and I see Andrew, standing nearby dancing with a girl catch my eye, telepathically nodding in agreement as if I asked him why the pool was open, then the two shirtless girls jump into the pool and the crowd roars with approval. One surfaces, her nipples visible through her thin pink brassiere, dancing on the steps leading out of the pool, hands resting on her knees, ass shaking to the music. An adventurous fellow quickly kicks off his shoes and steps into the water, his jeans wet up to his knees, grabs her and starts pounding her right there. The girl acquiesces to his advance, grabbing a guide rail by the steps and the DJ screams *Yeeaaah pool party now!* For some reason people start throwing cups into the pool and within minutes, the shallow end is filled with revelers, some fully clothed. I leave the debacle, seeing Ed dancing maniacally with a girl beside Bolt, squeeze past the section where Flame and his entourage are, covered in a thick cloud of weed smoke filled with guys making virtual gun salutes with their hands, Flame in an unusually dark corner with Cynthia, face to face dancing together, then I go to the other side of the dance deck, where it seems every girl has thrown away their inhibitions. One girl in a white skirt, is holding on to the trunk of one of the large potted palms, the tree shaking in a frenzy of motion as a guy behind her hits her ass with his crotch like a piston, beside him two girls give lap dances to guys sitting in chairs, chairs that I saw earlier in Andrew's parents living room. Beside them, girls dance with girls, puffing fat spliffs and doing alternating shots of Patrón. One of the chairs collapses from the frolicking, an event which causes the people around erupt in laughter. The fallen guy doesn't move, simply resting his elbows on the ground as the girl adjusts position to continue dancing with him, her skirt hiked up and her black panties visible to the world. I leave the deck, go towards the bar, where Brittany stops me and gives me a look I know too well, but I squeeze her hand, walking past Eric, who is asleep beside some boxes at the bar, see Valerie dancing waist to waist with Chris, who seemed to magically teleport from the poolside here, and stand near the entrance, where Beckford has vanished and someone scribbled "YEAH YEAH YEAH" on the paper with the names of people on the list. The line of cars on the street in front of Andrew's house seem to stretch forever, parked on all the front lawns of every resident for half a mile. A Nissan Sentra across the road is shaking to and fro, its heavily tinted windows hiding its frisky occupants. The crowd roars again, and I look up to the sky, cloudless but dark, then go back inside, towards the kitchen, where I see Berlin in the hallway, unaware of me as she looks at the same painting Amy and Kwame Anthony had been admiring earlier. A guy from the kitchen lumbers past her, smiling lecherously and says something, his eyes thick with intent. She gives him a gentle nod and whispers something I cannot hear, but this satisfies the man and he walks past me, his eyes still heavy with lust, heavy with a need to find a girl tonight, and I walk up to Berlin.

"A man just got rejected," I say to her.

Without turning in my direction, she says, "A man just asked to eat my pussy, a man I do not know."

"A man needs to know you to be a cunning linguist?" I ask.

"If a man wants my 'pum pum' there are standards he must follow," she says.

Another loud, powerful laugh erupts from my system.

"Standards."

"Yes look here," she says, pointing at the painting.

"It's like this painting here, you see this woman, standing in a seemingly submissive stance. We feel like the voyeurs here, as she holds what appears to be a towel too scanty to cover her body. Her back is towards us, most of it uncovered, with the towel barely hiding her ass—which is fantastic by the way—and her left breast. We can assume that she is the one being observed, the one caught in the act, a moment frozen in time for us to enjoy ad infinitum."

"How does this relate to a guy wanting to go down on you?"

"What is her standard? How do you know that she didn't beguile the painter into making this image? How do you know that she didn't force him to do it after a night of dirty, sweaty sex? Isn't it possible that this image of supposed naivety, of us seeing her in a vulnerable moment is not vulnerable at all? This could have been all part of her elaborate plan, a plan to be immortalized so people would admire her ass and wonder how her tits look?"

She turns to me, running a finger across my collarbone.

"How do you know, it wasn't that she didn't want a guy to go down on her, but it was probably just… the wrong guy?"

She is painfully close, and her breath, smelling sweetly of Vodka and cranberry juice, slides into my nostrils. I feel the stirrings of an erection in my pants.

"Something tells me we aren't talking about the woman in the painting anymore," I say in a heavy breath.

"A man is observant," she says, moving inches away from my face.

Then, I hear the music get very low and concerned, I excuse myself from Berlin, go outside and see several armed men in bullet proof jackets holding assault rifles standing by the pool, police.

"Looks like the party is over people!" comes the voice of the DJ. "But I hear that after this everyone is heading to Club Intrigue! So from Inside to Intrigue we go!"

An officer taps the DJ, whispers something into his ear, and he stops the music immediately. Bodies are streaming out of the venue, dozens of people in various stages of inebriation. Men speaking loudly and walking with bottles in their hands, girls barefoot holding their heels in their hands, laughing at nothing. The roar of engines and cars driving too fast on the crowded street is the new noise, the new din. Then I remember Berlin and my heart beats quickly, thinking of her face close to mine, the seductive look in her eyes. I walk back into the kitchen, but she isn't there. Outside, the deck is emptying, the tables previously surrounded by celebrities now empty. Many of the bottles still full or half full.

Andrew and I work with the staff, collecting the remaining bottles, packing leftover Patrón, Grey Goose and Moet into boxes which will be kept in Andrew's basement, collapse the tables, move a few chairs inside, collapse the tables that the celeb groups were using and sweep up broken glass from different areas. The kitchen is in a significant state of disarray, with the fridge ajar, food missing and wet slices of bread on the counter. Stains from spilt liquor sprinkle the tiled floor, and the smell of Vokda and Pepsi lingers in the air. Boot and heel marks track through this sticky mess backwards and forwards, with a few heading into the living room and upstairs.

"The cleaners will deal with this tomorrow," Andrew says, rubbing Britney's stomach.

Britney looks tired but her eyes are still ready, glossy with the activity of the night, her body never more than three feet away from Andrew's. As I help to put some of the boxes of liquor in the basement, I think of Berlin's finger running across my collarbone and the raw intention in her eyes as she spoke about the painting. I feel the rush again, teasing blood slowly into my loins. Beside me Britney yawns, face devoid of concern. Outside, the area is now somewhat restored to its former glory, with the exception of a few broken potted plants on the major deck. The chill hits me full on in the face and goose bumps rise on my arms with the sight of Kingston in front of me, a Kingston still wide awake and down for whatever. I hear the boom of large wooden doors close behind me, and all is silent again, the bohemian energy of the party now a ghost of the past. A small, white Toyota van pulls in front of the house and most of the event staff pile into the vehicle with the exception of a staffer named David, who decides to accompany us to club Intrigue. Andrew isn't fit to drive and comes into the car with me, Britney and David. The streets morph from the rough asymmetrical shapes of roadways built on hills to the sharper edges of the city grid. Andrew is raving about the party and bursting at the seams with the potential of his renewed social capital via the endless pictures taken with celebrities and the knowledge that all these people would be blasting said pictures all over social media. The images of the night are a mixed blur of context as I keep driving, mostly nodding as he speaks freely about the sexy women, including those he has an interest in. I glance at Britney in the rear view mirror, smiling to herself and unaffected by Andrew's ramblings. A quick memory of wanting to enter the void comes into the forefront of my mind, the moment I walked to the gate, as nothingness screamed at me from my glove compartment. Thinking of Berlin, I feel a warmth in me, a trickle of something I believe was buried. Expectancy.

We pull in front of the club, and I feel my heart tremble again, knowing she is somewhere in there. A man directs us into V.I.P parking, where I am directed into position beside another black Range Rover with customized wheels. I walk out with the group in tow, Andrew with his arm around Britney, sneaking kisses, David looking fresh after a night of busy work. I see the sign for the spot, an 'I' designed in a gothic English font glowing purple. A dense crowd of late night revelers waits in line in to pay and get in, some of whom I recognize from my party. I gesture with my arms and excuse myself through the throng, nodding at both security guards who are tall men built like farmhouses, pectorals stretching their undersized shirts, which read "INTRIGUE SECURITY". Everyone walks in, including an enthusiastic David, who keeps shaking my hand saying *Respect boss man!* I nod as we walk down the walkway.

Intrigue is a huge space in the belly of an old office building. Labyrinthine with its many corridors and walkways that lead to a central area, it is one of the most common after party spots in Kingston. Personally strippers don't intrigue me much (pun intended), and throwing money at women has never done anything to excite me. There is something sad and obvious about a strip club, more naked than the women parading on stage. Something embedded in the walls where porn runs on repeat on large LCD screens, where the women are always thirsty for a glass of champagne, and men with fat wallets sit back in V.I.P sections, waving happily to girls who give blow-jobs for two thousands dollars and have sex for five. Tonight is a full house. I can barely see in front of my face as people stand to attention, watching the stage, where six girls dance in various positions, vertical or inverted. Someone grabs my arm, and I see Chris with Valerie. She gives me a drunk smile, reaching out to touch my arm but misses by a mile. He slaps something heavily into my palm then pulls her quickly away, through the crowd and towards one of the four bars in each corner of the central area. In my hand is a stack of thousand dollar bills. From the size I can assume it is at least forty thousand Jamaican dollars. Andrew calls my name and we all move adjacent to the stage, where we walk into V.I.P, seeing Flame, Bolt, Baby Cham, Sean Paul and most of the celebs from the previous party, each person with a table filled with fresh bottles of premium liquor. Ed is also there, with a new girl by his side, a grin on his face as he hands me a bottle of Hennessy.

"Drink!" he shouts, immediately turning and giving the girl, who is seated, a lap dance.

I get a glass and hand one to David, who doesn't want any chaser, and pour him some Hennessy. In quick succession, he says hello to the celebrities present, who all give him hearty hellos. The DJ screams on the microphone.

"Yow I just heard that the party *Inside* was EPIC! Make sure next time you invite yours truly, DJ Live to the party!"

Andrew makes a weak noise that sounds like a cheer, his face looking flat but cheerful as Britney gives him an energetic lap dance. Whatever fatigue she had before is gone. I take a light sip of the Hennessy, coughing at the burn it produces, when someone else taps me on the shoulder, a man dressed in a Human Made Yokosuka Jumper. He slaps a wad of money into my hand, this stack of thousands even bigger than the one Chris gave me. I open my mouth to ask him who it was from, but he smiles, saying *Everything good boss, Everything good.*

I give some of the money to Andrew, who immediately throws most of it in the wrong direction, into the crowd, followed by Ed.

"Make it rain bitches! Make it rain!" Ed says, throwing wads of cash.

People in the crowd, mostly women, snatch up the freely flying dollar bills when the entire V.I.P section starts tossing money at the crowd and the stage, the strobe lights bouncing off the bills like fireflies in the night. The DJ screams and strippers grab the money, and dance more fervently. I give some of the bills to David, who immediately disappears with a stripper built like a horse into one of the private rooms. I take in the entire scene of flying money, men watching strippers on stage or dancing with strippers, women getting lap dances, and one adventurous guy pouring a bottle of champagne on a naked stripper, the foamy liquid running down between her breasts and over her cleanly shaved vagina. In the midst of the melee, I see Berlin, looking directly at me, to the slight left of the V.I.P area. She walks towards me, the strobe lights making her skin a deep purple, black lights giving her glowing green teeth and eyes. She leads me to the very back of my section, easing me onto a couch, resting her lips on my neck. The erection I have next is brutal, the kind from a place of stone cold sobriety. In synch with pounding, visceral dancehall music, she grinds on me slowly, relaxed, tossing her hair back and smiling at me. I'm trying to speak but she stops me, resting her index finger on my lips, enjoying herself. I lean back, taking it in, the noise behind me, and Berlin in front of me, her unapologetic press against my member, shifting it right and left in my pants. She takes my phone from my pocket and punches in her number, still gyrating her hips the entire time, sending erotic waves through me. My mind is on fire, wanting her right there, all of her. I want to see her naked, to smell her hair and taste her skin against my lips and be inside her, thrusting into a predictable conclusion. She slips the phone back into my pocket and leans into me, filling my nostrils with the same sweet fragrance I'd detected earlier, and says:

"A man needs to call me tomorrow."

Berlin gets up and walks away quickly, out of the V.I.P and back into the crowd as I sit there, erection straining against my pants, heart racing. I whip out the phone and scroll down, seeing, 'BERLIN' as a new entry, the profile photo my face with my eyes closed, taken while she was dancing with me, I smile and look at the message over and over, hanging on to the tingle in my system.

Chapter Ten

Berlin and I sit at a Café somewhere in Barbican, the kind that serves jumbo lattes and three hundred dollar oatmeal and raisin cookies. I like the décor, with its brown and white finish on everything, cups adorned with the logo of a smiling girl with short curly hair, purposely small tables to fit more patrons and the posters of vintage strongmen, clowns and dancers placed in no real order all around the venue. A Wurlitzer replica jukebox is in the corner, tubes glowing, oddly playing some kind of house music mix. I look at it for a moment, seeing the coin slot that fits American quarters, wondering about that time period, of young men driving long automobiles with their greased hair, with girls in frilly dresses in the passenger seats as the radio probably plays Elvis, things like Doo Wop and a world of celebrities like Harry Belafonte, Frank Sinatra and Ella Fitzgerald. Such realities continue to be a far cry from what I imagine Kingston in the fifties to be, filled with open-air spots where people listened to Ska music or chill reggae under a warm sky. The girl taking orders looks bored and flips through a copy of *Fear and Loathing in Las Vegas,* her eyes making brief contact with mine as she takes my money, gives me a receipt and tells me in a yawn that it will be a ten minute wait for our food. I walk back outside, feeling the hanging chill in the air, and sit down. In front of me, Berlin is flipping through a tattered copy of an old Vogue magazine, her hair out today, down to her shoulders, her eyes hidden behind a large pair of John Varvatos eyeglasses. She's wearing a thin black cardigan, a white tank top, dark grey shorts that stop mid-thigh, and the same grey Dr. Martens boots.

"I like your glasses," I say to her.

"I'm feeling manly today," she replies with a smile, briefly tilting the magazine down and smiling at me.

The smile injects me with the same feeling of anticipation I experienced before going to the club the night before and I feel my face flush briefly, cutting the chill around me. The same serving girl comes over to our table, bringing two cups of hot Coffee, walking away without saying anything else. I sip on the hot liquid, watching Berlin read her magazine, noticing how relaxed her shoulders are, her left folded leg under the table slightly brushing mine but not moving. A few minutes pass, time that holds me in a simple grip, unencumbered by idle thoughts. Berlin puts down the magazine.

"What do you think about celebrity?" she asks, peering into her cup of coffee before putting it to her lips.

She slides off her glasses, revealing her eyes.

"What kind of celebrity? The kind of celebrity one is born with, or the kind thrust upon people?" I ask.

"Isn't it the same thing?"

"Not really, but I think celebrity is an interesting societal tool," I say.

"Really, a tool? Like the one dangling between your legs?"

I smile, replying. "No, I think celebrities have use. We idolize them and forget about our petty little lives, want to be like them, like ourselves more if we resemble them, and in knowing them, can have more access to things, people and places instead of just being ourselves."

"I see. So the plebeians live petty little lives eh? Aren't most celebrities the ones dying of overdoses, publicly collapsing under the weight of their own success and so watched and hawked on by the media that being idolized is some kind of unending nightmare?"

"This is true. I guess the context is different in Jamaica," I say.

"It is quite different here."

"Jamaican culture tends to favourably accept people with relative bravado and confidence. It is unusual for a person to have the sort of fanaticism for a celebrity that one might have in say, America or Japan. You see the famous people everywhere so often, there is no thrill to chasing them down and snapping pictures."

"What about tangential celebrity? Perceived things that give you a sense of celebrity?"

She looks at me, her face slightly serious, coffee cup to her lips. I lean back in my chair.

"You mean like being sort of famous," I say.

"Or not even famous at all, but famous anyways."

"Explain."

She rests the coffee cup on the table, and I feel her unfold her legs from under the table as she sits upright.

"The number of men that proposition me here is incredible," she says with a smile.

"I guess we are talking about 'white celebrity' then."

"White celebrity?"

"This is a post-colonial society. The social stratas tend to end up top with the palest kind."

"I see, but do you find that weird, these ideas, these ideologies?"

I fold my arms, tilting my head to the right.

"Well, I guess I have a perspective on it, but growing up here, it simply *is*. I try not to ascribe to too many things involving all that hegemonic ideology."

"But here you are with a white girl."

I laugh.

"A white girl who invited me out."

She giggles and rubs my leg under the table.

"I'm serious though, if I was to really be a scatterbrained wanderlust, coming to Jamaica looking for nothing but a good time in bed and men to take me out, I'd have a full plate," she says, looking behind me, inside the eatery.

"How long have you been here?" I ask.

"Just a few days, but I'm already fielding several offers from several men to do several things," she says matter-of-factly.

"Things like what?"

"Let's see. Three offers to go to Portland this weekend, two invitations to dinner at the same restaurant in Marketplace, a street dance downtown, a short film premiere, a trip to Montego Bay and a trip to Ocho Rios."

"Are you serious?"

"Does the Pope like missionary?" she asks, standing up.

I pause, thinking, as she walks inside. Behind me I hear her talking to the server, asking about the food. She sits back down.

"It's been thirteen minutes and I'm very hungry."

"So… the Pope."

"Oh, that. Naturally the Pope doesn't like missionary, at least, I hope he doesn't, but yes, I was being quite serious."

She speaks in a light, disinterested way.

"So… these offers you are fielding…," I start.

"Am I seriously considering any of them you ask?"

She rubs my leg under the table again, her fingers drifting a few inches higher than the previous time.

"A woman is constantly considering everything, but what does that mind of yours tell you?"

I rub my forehead, about to respond when the cashier appears with two plates, both carrying large sandwiches with sides of French fries and small trays with sour cream and ketchup.

"Do you have juice?" Berlin asks the girl, who is already trying to walk away.

"Yes," the girl replies.

"Do you mind telling me what kind?"

"We have fruit juice, like Guava, Mango... that kind of thing."

"I'll take a glass of Guava juice. Indie?"

"I'll have the same."

The girl disappears and Berlin immediately bites into the sandwich, voraciously tearing at it with her teeth, grabbing fries at random.

"Oh this is like a mouth orgasm," she says to me, left cheek puffed out with unchewed food. "So, you didn't answer my question."

In the middle of chewing my sandwich, I raise an index finger and swallow.

"Logic dictates that a girl fielding so many offers would simply choose what she wants to do. Depending on her personality, what impresses or offends her, she would pick an outing with an outcome she considers the most favourable relative to her needs in that moment."

"Which brings us here, today," she says, smiling. "So don't worry your pretty little head about it. But back to our little chat about celebrity, I feel so famous here! Everywhere I go, I get into V.I.P pretty easily or people bring me into V.I.P for no other reason that I'm a cute white girl, and then once they hear I'm German a lot of the men get ecstatic and start tossing drinks at me and offers involving far away hotels and devouring vaginas."

I sputter a laugh into my drink.

"How many men have propositioned you in that way?"

"Just two, but that never happens to me in Germany. Some guy I don't know, just coming up to me and asking to eat my pussy? Jamaica is insane!"

I smile at her, biting into my sandwich again, marveling at whatever is unfolding in front of me.

"The Jamaican taboos are fading," I say, wiping my mouth.

"I think they faded for you a long time ago," she says, flashing a seductive smile.

The rush hits me in the groin again, and I feel myself swelling, insistent, needing her. A part of me feels strange, a fractured sense of comfort with the pieces slowly coming together.

"I don't think we'd be here if I fielded you an offer to eat your special place," I say, taking a final bite of my sandwich.

"And how do *you* know that I didn't want that in the first place?"

She looks at me without smiling, her eyes serious and involved. The gaze in its intensity holds me for a few seconds, before she breaks into a laugh.

"Oh my god, I totally had you! You really think I'm some kind of freak don't you?"

"No I don't," I reply hastily, my palms a little sweaty.

Berlin looks at her cell phone.

"I have to leave soon to meet Marta somewhere. So you have t-minus two minutes to throw your offer on the table."

"My offer?"

"Yes, of social engagement, good times, preferably those involving alcohol and the possible resolution of initial sexual tensions in the glorious release of coitus."

Something is both frightened and warm inside me. I shuffle nervously in my seat.

"There is a party tonight, and open air kind of vibe, we can go there," I say.

"Sounds like a plan, and look, here is Wynton."

A white Isuzu station wagon pulls into the parking lot, coming to a stop directly behind us. The driver, a stocky man with thick patches of hair on his neck smiles at Berlin as she waves to him. Getting up, she walks over to me and rubs my head.

"Later tonight then," she says.

"Yes," I say with a smile.

She hops into the taxi and waves at me as it drives off, the muffler gurgling out white smoke. I see her in the taxi wondering what she is feeling in this moment, thinking of what it is like to be her, shooting those calm beams of energy out into the universe, as men come up to her, seeing those striking eyes and face, that tall, lithe body bundled up with her unique brain. This makes me concerned, this idea of her potentiality. That smile and that quirky sensibility, it must be infectious. I don't see just a few men fielding offers, I see them all asking her to go everywhere, to all the restaurants to all the beaches, strip clubs and cool spots. My brain drifts somewhere else, into a life where we were together. We'd talk on the phone every other day and send each other regular e-mails, the kind filled with smiley faced emoticons and selfies taken in odd locations, and I'd juggle going to Germany every six months and she'd do the same, coming on her holiday breaks to Jamaica from a life I'm not fully briefed on yet. We'd hang out in buildings that still have the marks of war on them, drink different kinds of beer and laugh as we kiss in the middle of a crowd during Oktoberfest, both of us wearing Lederhosen and long white socks. I'd hang with her friends, who would be just as cool as she is, speaking fluent English with a quirky sensibility about reality, the kind that comes from specific areas of academia like philosophical studies, art history and anthropology. We'd smoke weed around a bonfire in an abandoned basement, wearing jackets to cut the nip of the pre-winter weather, someone's radio behind us playing music from a hip German radio station. The guys there, Berlin and her friends would laugh at something the radio DJ says, and she'd translate it for me, rubbing my thigh and giving me a kiss on the cheek when I get a little embarrassed because my German isn't fluent yet, but I'd hold her hand and it would be enough, she'd be everything and we'd be two parts of a whole. Our outfits would even be similar on that night, my fresh pair of Dr. Martens boots an inspired purchase on a late night stroll down some street with a hard to pronounce name, where the topic of boots and candy leads to hours of uproarious laughter and passionate admittances of things we love about each other. Her body wouldn't be a mysterious, undiscovered place that I'd never seen or touched. It wouldn't be a thing of conjecture and fantasy. I would know the weight and slope of her breasts, how soft her skin felt against mine. I'd know all her tastes and moods. We'd lie down in the morning in her flat, saying nothing at all, while I do things on my Macbook Air and she checks her e-mail on her iPad. Possibly I'd try and bring *Inside* to the city of Berlin, or some derivative of it. She, with her savvy and connections, would set me up with the right people, people that love Jamaica and Jamaicans. We'd get a space in an old warehouse, a German wunderkind of the art community would design our fliers and promotional material and as the buzz started to pickup, I'd be improving in my German classes and more able to engage with her friends. I'd go around town by myself, ordering lunch and reading through the newspaper, Kingston a distant memory. But on the occasions we swap countries, we'd still live an interesting life. I'd watch her tan on a beach in Negril and smile at me as I take pictures of her eating fried fish and festivals. We'd be hanging with Andrew and whoever his new flame of the month was, all of us laughing and smiling, looking out on the blue-green water, the kind that feels like a warm bath on a warm day, perfection stretching out onto the horizon. Things would change about me internally; I'd see the value in a relationship past the boundaries I'd barely crossed before. There would be less of a need to rage and chase through life. I'd be walking at a normal pace, taking in all in the sights, sounds and the things around me. She'd be there, behind it all, teaching me new little things every now and then about snacks like Currywurst and Matjesbrötchen. There'd be the nights we'd probably fight and I'd go to some hotel down the road, and she'd call me, crying, telling me to come back to her place, but then she'd end up at the hotel and we'd be naked and going at it in the shower, water burning our steaming bodies, our minds reset to the task of making each other feel as good as possible, lying down and waking up looking into each others eyes, saying nothing. My first winter in Germany would be terrible. I'd curse at the brutal cold and she'd laugh at my pea coat, which would be stylish, some brand like Yves Saint Laurent, but it would be too thin and unsuitable for the real winter. She'd tell me about the wonderful world of thermal underclothing and proper boots and we'd trudge through snow-covered ground to go to a hip club, and I'd lose myself in the moment as lights flashed over our heads and she wore something like a white halter top and leather pants, me, her and her friends, all raging with fists to the sky, dance music feeding this image, pushing me deeper into a reality where she exists. I'd wake up one day and realize I'd fallen for her in a way I can't imagine, that the core of my being is now linked to who she is. I'd have her picture as the background of my phone, and one day while I'm taking a person's information relating to brand sponsorship for another edition of *Inside: Berlin,* they'd see her picture on my phone and ask her if she is my girlfriend, and I'd say yes, a genuine smile on my face with nothing but the future on my mind.

The taxi is gone now and I wonder what I'm thinking, all these thoughts about a girl I just met.

* * * *

I'm back at the parking lot party, sitting in the car, today wearing a festive yellow Dolce & Gabanna Togolese Republic shirt, grey Evisu jeans and grey suede shoes. The drink in my hand makes a hissing noise as I add more soda and chaser to my cup, which I rest in the cup holder facing the radio. Two girls wearing formal dresses and high heels stroll through the parking lot in stark contrast to the atmosphere. Behind them, men dressed in matching jeans jackets and fitted caps that read "YMCMB" walk behind them, gesturing confidently as they talk about something I will never hear. The radio is playing Fire 105.7 and Gytpian's "Be Alright" is blasting into my ear in a progressive Auto-Tune crescendo. A sleek Benz pulls into the parking lot, the driver a very dark skinned man wearing wire-rimmed glasses. He honks indignantly at a security guard, coming to a stop near a hazard cone protecting parking spots for VIPs. I can see their conversation play out without needing to hear words. The security guard is paid to tell people they cannot park where the cones are, the man with his Benz and designer glasses will tell the guard he can park anywhere. The dialogue goes back and forth a few times, and I see the security guard's resolve slowly weaken. The man he is speaking to is driving a car that after shipping costs and import taxes costs upwards of one hundred and fifty thousand U.S dollars. A man like that by his virtue must be someone, I see the guard thinking, his shoulders now slightly drooped as the man speaks to him in a calm, practiced manner. The man in the Benz has done this dozens of times in dozens of scenarios. An overriding status leaks out through the windows of the man's car, covering the security guard in a thick fog of self-doubt. Then the battle is over, the guard moves the cone, the Benz driving quickly into the parking space. More guys walk in, one in camouflage pants, a black tank top, red belt and air force ones, beside a fellow with a heavily bleached face wearing a floral print shirt, green Capris and lace less shoes. Two tall girls, presumably models, walk by in designer black pants and high top Chuck Taylors, one with the left side of her head shaved, diamond cross earrings glistening from both earlobes. Near the entrance, I see a woman with a shaved head in a tiger pattern body dress and gold wrap sandals laugh with a giant of a man in a black shirt one size too small who is drinking a cup of soup from one of the outside vendors. I keep taking in the people in their various sizes and shapes, moving by in slow motion in my mind, as I take sips of my drink, the radio now playing "Whine and Kotch" by Charly Black. I'm waiting on Berlin to arrive. She's taking a cab, having politely declined my request to pick her up, wherever it is she's staying. A brief image of her from earlier in the day comes to mind, her reading the Vogue magazine, sun lightly hitting her skin. I swallow some more liquor, almost laughing at a man in comically tight lime green pants and a black shirt, walk with his meager chest puffed out. This moment of humour fades quickly as I recognize Berlin walking in beside a man who is more recognizable than she is.

She is walking with Kwame Anthony.

Chapter Eleven

The paranoia is palpable. My system surges as a flurry of images hit my mind. I see her and him naked or not, in a car or in a bed. She is moaning and lightly covered in sweat, he is grunting in pleasure. Beside her, the phone rings with my phone call, but no one answers. The scenario is always true in this Kingston town, the obviousness of the frantic frolicking that takes place so often. The cards are dealt and one must deal with them, but I don't want it to be true. I see her eyes looking at me with concern as she stops in the middle of a laugh. There is no guilt there, just surprise at seeing me and she comes over. With no foreknowledge of what is happening my reaction is unjust, I know, but I feel annoyed anyway. I am not a possessive person. There is no need for this gradually increasing wave of anger rising in my stomach. I am not a jealous person, I do not need to deal with the dull rationale that comes with an overzealous expectation of what a person deserves. Normally I feel nothing, and stimulation comes from few, dangerous sources. This though, this feeling she is giving me, feels more dangerous than my cocktails and wild nights out. This sensation of losing her, feeling her slip away so soon feels tragic. She steps closer and I wonder why time is so warped with her around me, why her aura makes me tremble. Why does she make me question things, is the main question on my mind. I am not a person who feels things, but now it seems, that is changing.

"Hey Indie," she says to me.

"Berlin," I reply. "How do you know Kwame Anthony?"

She rests a hand on my shoulder.

"Isn't he hot? Me and my friend took a picture with him a week ago at Weddy Wednesdays. He remembered me so he said hello when I was walking in."

"I bet he remembers a lot of girls," I say with a sigh, looking away.

"What, are you jealous my little munchkin?"

"Jealousy is for people with emotions."

"Hume said humans are slaves to emotions," she remarks, poking me in the stomach, adding: "Slavery is over. Besides I think you are sexy."

Blood rushes to my loins and I feel myself wanting her again all at once.

"Really?"

"You not being sexy is like Chuck Norris not doing round-house kicks," she says assertively.

The laugh that leaves me is the loudest I can remember making in recent history. My stomach trembles with convulsions and it becomes difficult to breathe. I look up at her and she smiles and I feel warm and accepted. She is wearing a large black belt, a short black skirt and a white sleeveless top with a printed image of a man wearing three different coloured hats. The slight press of her breasts against the fabric kick starts the feeling of another erection, and I shake my head to get into focus, watching Kwame Anthony pose with two girls for a photo. They walk away, giggling to themselves, while he stands there, eyes looking on the horizon. He could be thinking about pussy, taking a shit or putting the finishing touches on his new album. The man is unreadable.

Then I think of him and Amy, her arms resting on his shoulder as they looked at the painting, the non-committal expression on her face as she spoke to me. This from a woman who at one point insisted on giving me daily blowjobs. Kwame Anthony smirks to himself, chuckling about something and I see Amy between his legs, humming one of his songs as she gives him head, tugging on the locks drifting way past his shoulders, on some expensive leather couch in a house like mine, somewhere on a hill like the one I live on.

"Where are you?" comes the voice of Berlin.

She is looking at me, her face masked in the shadow of what one could call concern, but I label as lingering curiosity.

"I'm here," I reply.

My heart jumpstarts with recognition as Amy walks in, along with a woman that is quite possibly the most attractive I've ever seen. She is ridiculously tall and voluptuous, with the dark skin of a person used to a life of tanning on the beach. Her hair is long, black and luxurious. Her eyes, powerfully sensuous, scan the area we are in quickly, settling on Kwame Anthony. Her full lips break into a car-stopping smile. She walks over and gives him a long hug, his reaction modest and simple, as if he was hugging his sister. Seeing Amy makes my hands tremble again, and I walk to the bar, saying hello to two fellows who shout "Epic! Epic!" at me in reference to the *Inside* party, shake the hand of a friend of the DJ who was playing that night, nod at Tristan, who looks worried about something but I don't ask him what, and a friend of Connie's, Elizabeth, who is mostly on her phone, rapidly typing on a messaging program. I get a bottle of rum and some chasers, not before seeing Gregory, the banker, who tells me about some people hanging out at Devon House that I should talk to about hosting an event, I tap Ricardo, who is walking with his camera today and snaps a photo of me and a girl I don't know, then go back over to Berlin and the group which has now swelled to eight people. I gesture to one of the waiting staff to get a table, but I realize a table is already there with two bottles of rum in buckets of ice. Resting my bottle beside the other two, I quickly fix myself a drink and look to Berlin, who already has one, raising her glass in 'cheers' to me as a tall fellow with a short head of locks smiles and chats with her. Amy hasn't said anything to me, her arm in the crook of Kwame's arm as he throws superstar daggers into the eye of the bombshell brunette. My head swims into the memory of the guy she was seeing when she was seeing me, a guy who is still short, now fat and happily married with two children. The vision swims and I'm paddling through the emotions I felt then, the rage, the shock, the depression. Then I go deeper into the swimming pool, and I'm looking at my house on the horizon of my memory, and I'm at a dinner party my parents had.

There were twenty to thirty guests slated to come to the house. I wasn't older than seven or eight, running around causing mischief as the adults dined and drank, chatting about politics, the day's Jamaica Gleaner headlines and other things I didn't understand in my child mind. My father had invited a branch manager for one of his businesses to the party, a buxom half Chinese woman named Yvette that even I at seven years old found remarkably attractive. She came to the party in a body fitting black dress and red heels, to the chagrin of my mother, who spent the evening giving her icy stares in between political anecdotes. I wasn't at the table really, just unable to sleep because the dinner party started at eight, but as I scampered about, I took in all the details around me as little children do. My father had constantly laughed and slapped the shoulder of a man beside him while intermittently giving Yvette nudges on her shoulder and frequent winks. Yvette would blush and then immediately my mother would laugh and go into another story about something else, the crowd following her quickly, the wine, beer and rum making them perfect attention deficit targets. Eventually after the food was finished, people were milling about outside, chatting and laughing in the dark of the evening time. My father was sitting at a table with Yvette and a few of his business associates. I was peering through the window of my bedroom, and I could see the one or two times he lightly ran his finger across her hand while he was gesturing strongly to the men at the table with a fixed gaze. Uncertainty about something rippled through my child body, a questioning discomfort about the dynamics of what was happening. However, I didn't have much time to question whatever I was thinking because the nature of such dynamics would forever be understood by me in the next few minutes. Idly alternating between playing with a few G.I Joe action figures and reading tattered X-men comics I heard my mother's voice. She was calling me, and I left the explosive battlefield of plush carpeting and ran downstairs. She was standing by the door to her office, and as I approached, took me in with stern eyes.

"Knock twice if you see him coming towards this room," she said to me.

I sulked and nodded, waiting by the door for about ten minutes, which in child time is an eternity. Eventually the door opened, and I saw my mother and the man she was sitting beside for most of the dinner come out. The man had a smirk on his face and beads of sweat on his forehead, and my mother wiped her lips with the back of her hand, her eyes filled with dark mischief. With the same hand, she patted me on the forehead.

"Good job," she said to me, as she walked over to the table and poured another glass of wine from the bottle for herself. My father had come into the living room soon afterward, being greeted heartily by the man who was in the room with my mother. She had smiled then, a smile that looked greedy and dangerous and I had felt afraid, sincerely afraid, going to my room and not leaving until everyone had gone. The details were unclear in that moment, but I knew that something had happened. Something hurtful and done on purpose, something glowing hot and bright between the grey areas of whatever kind of love my parents had. The way my mother had looked at my father then, with both a smile and hate in her eyes, her lips shiny under the light of the living room.

I'm brought back to reality by the noise of feedback from the microphone the DJ is holding in his hand.

"Ground control to major Indie," came the voice of Berlin.

I look at her, smiling.

"Where did you go?" she asks.

"I'm right here," I reply, pinching her left shoulder.

"No, you weren't. I can see you were somewhere else, just like the night I met you."

"Just thinking about a few things," I say.

"Like you were at the party? What were you thinking about?"

I shrug my shoulders, replying, "Nothing important."

"Where do you live?" she asks.

"Somewhere between Jack's Hill and Beverly Hills," I reply, swallowing the last of my drink.

I reach for my bottle and pour myself another drink as someone in the group eyes me warily, and whispers something to Kwame Anthony.

"Do you live with your parents?"

"No, they kicked the bucket a while back," I reply.

"You mean they are dead?"

"Deep in the ground probably frowning at my lifestyle. Though my mother loved to drink as much as I do, maybe even more so."

"That's not funny," Berlin says, her smile gone.

For a second guilt wells inside me. I cannot remember the last time I have spoken about my parents.

"There is nothing more on this earth that I love more than my parents," she says, her voice gaining a rising indignance. "I cannot believe you would so casually refer to them dying like it was nothing."

"I didn't say it was no—"

"Forget about it," Berlin replies, walking away.

I feel like reaching for her, walking her down and trying to talk, but I let her go away. The next drink I make is much stronger, with less chaser and down it in a quick gulp but it has no effect on me, other than making my mouth burn.

"Yo boss, are you bothering that girl?" comes an unfamiliar voice.

It is the man with the short locks who was speaking to Berlin earlier.

"Really?" I ask, without looking at him.

"What you mean really? I see you by our table making drinks, but I don't know who you are."

"I don't know who you are either, so we are in the same boat," I reply, pouring more rum into my glass and getting ice from the tray.

The man's left eye squints with annoyance as he watches me make the drink.

"Listen to me—"

"You can stop," I say with a sigh. "This bottle right here, see it? I bought it. Obviously we have mutual friends at this table so please, just relax. You think I'd just walk up to your table, actually *his* table and start mixing drinks if I didn't know anyone here? Does that make any sense to you?"

"No, but—"

"Yes but you *assumed* I didn't know anyone here. Why?"

I sigh and pick my bottle up off the table.

"He's cool," comes the crystal clear voice of Kwame Anthony behind us. "It was his vibe we went to last night up at the big house."

"His party was the *Inside* party?" the man with the short locks says to Kwame Anthony.

"Yeah man, he's a good youth," Kwame Anthony says.

Kwame Anthony's voice immediately diffuses any tension around us and the man now seems ready to smile and hug me, but Amy seems even more enamored by Kwame Anthony and I walk away with the bottle, annoyed, looking for another spot. I go to a shadowy wall near a loudspeaker and close my eyes, feeling the music vibrate my earlobes. People keep flowing into the party in a steady stream. In the middle bodies move in unison, stepping perfectly to the rhythm of the music. A few bodies are pressed tightly into dark corners, grinding to a different beat. Many of the young men walk around with smiles on their faces, more guys in tight pants and a mix of t-shirts with garish prints. I see the hand slaps of people greeting each other, girls trying to look cute but looking silly and dance crews warming up to try and dominate the dance floor.

"You are really bad at this," comes the voice of Berlin.

I break out of my trance, my eyes slightly glazed with a thin coating of liquor.

"I guess so," I reply nonchalantly.

"A woman storms off, a man should follow her."

"A man might be afraid of getting slapped in the face," I say.

"Silly bird," she says, stepping close to me, her waist touching mine.

Her body feels nice next to mine. As I lean forward and dance with her, her hair brushes my lips and tickles the nape of my neck. Her eyes intermittently look at me, sly and alluring. I give her a quick twirl, surprising her. She smiles broadly, a little embarrassed, showing even rows of clear white teeth. Again I feel myself melting in her presence. I sneak moves as we dance; a quick run of my hand down her back, a playful tap on her forehead during a turn. This makes her smile more and dance faster, as if to dissuade me from further pranks. I forget about everything around me, including Amy and when she asks me to come on a hike to the Blue Mountain with her the next day, I say yes, kissing her neck softly, breaking it away as more bodies spill into the party, making it thicker and darker, like the night sky.

* * * *

It is interesting to me that I have never been to the Blue Mountains. They have always been in the background ever looming and silent, but they have never called to me. Where I live is quiet and verdant enough and the idea of going to the peak of the mountains was never on my list. But with Berlin there is a purpose to the moment, something insistent and pertinent about the journey. The passage to the mountains we will take might be a passage to something else, but what exactly, I don't know. She tells me over the phone that Marta and a fellow named Mario will accompany us on the trip. We are taking the route from Mavis Bank to Papine.

I'm with Berlin and the group in a taxi, my car at my house. Berlin's eyes gleam with excitement as we drive up the winding roads leading to Mavis Bank.

"How come you have never been to the mountain before?" asks Mario.

"I guess it is always there, waiting to be climbed," I reply.

Most of the drive is silent, save the rumbling of something in the back of the taxi that needs repair. The heavy scent of the atmosphere kicks my nostrils into gear. Near Mavis Bank, we meet our guide, a man called Curry. He tells us we are taking Sheldon Trail first, and that the way isn't very short, and that we'll be stopping at Whitefield Hall when night falls, heading out early to catch the sunrise at the peak. Like the rest of the group, I'm wearing weather friendly jeans, hiking boots and a backpack with food items, a flashlight, raincoat and bottled water. After reaching Mavis Bank we walk up the road for some time before going onto the hillside. I look at Berlin. Her left wrist is filled with an assortment of silver bracelets and chains buttressed by a thick leather lanyard in the middle of them all. It makes no noise as we walk up the hillside, the sounds around us mostly the crunching of our footsteps on the stony ground, or the whoosh of the breeze through the trees. I walk behind Mario, Marta and Berlin, looking out onto the endless green landscape in front of me. The tour guide, occasionally making references to the plant life and random facts about Jamaican history, moves with the pointed steps of a man whose entire body is a rigid muscle. Everything about him is lean and sinewy, devoid of fat.

The environment is welcomingly blank and unfamiliar. Other than the usual scent of the leaves of familiar things like Almond trees, Mango trees and the occasional Orange trees, the terrain is a welcome step away from the Kingston deluge. There are no familiar faces lurking at every corner, no sharp noises or men hawking wares on dirty sidewalks as cars scream and honk behind them. The cool blanket of air hanging over us as we walk also holds something else, the release that true nature always seems to give human beings. I've never wondered why nature makes people introspective, and why being around trees and stretches of lush terrain make people shift into a different state. To me, the idea of a day-to-day life in a city is involved with the constant thinking and analyzing of things, people and places. Here there are no triggers to activate much thinking. A tree several hundred years old in front of me will be there until the roots die, unmoving and uncaring. The grass my feet trample will grow back every single time until a time when people won't walk on this path anymore, when the world is different and things like mountain hikes may not be necessary. Nature is a symbol of both eternity and finality I think, because it holds both death and endlessness within the seasonal adjustment of its environment. A mountain takes almost forever to erode, trees last the lifetimes of dozens of humans, and a stone, what some would call a dull, useless object can sit in the same place, and still be there millions of years later. The beginning and the end of it all is all around me. Maybe this creates serenity, or the illusion of serenity. But it doesn't matter, I realize. I like the cool air and the quiet around me, and so does my group it seems. No one is talking now, just glancing at the environment around themselves, the light echo of crunching feet the only thing speaking to the air.

Mario tells me a story about climbing the Dolomite Mountains in Italy. He was doing a lone hike and fell a few feet off the main path. He had to hobble back down for quite sometime in excruciating pain. He tells me that if his body didn't numb his leg, he wouldn't be here talking to me now. I agree with him. Trauma makes you numb to things, your body activates it and then it keeps you going as far as you need to, but at some time the pain will come back because it has to and then you cannot escape it but you thank your body for taking you so far. Berlin listens to our story but says nothing, smiling as she walks and takes in the nature around us, the sky darkening quickly as we approach Whitfield Hall, where we will spend the night.

The moon is clearly visible in the night sky, hanging over everything, watching elegantly above the backdrop of the dark terrain in front of me. I stare at it for a while; my arms pinched by the cold, the bed in my private room reasonably comfortable. But I am relaxed, lying down with the moon as my company. I'm drifting in and out of sleep, but not falling completely into the darkness. Eventually I sigh and stand up and walk by the window, ignoring the feeling of chilly wood on the undersides of my bare feet. A ripple of the feeling of serenity from the walk tickles me again as I see the moonlight casting reflections on thousands of leaves in the distance, many of them swaying slightly in an almost nonexistent breeze, dancing to a symphony only flora can hear. The world of those leaves and shadows, only illuminated by moonlight seems inviting and I want to go out there, walk between the leaves and feel them cool and soft, rubbing against my arms with the moonlight as my guide. Then, I hear a creak behind me. I turn to see Berlin standing in my room dressed in a long, dark grey robe. We stare at each other, my eyes fascinated by the moonlight's reflection on her skin and body, leaving half in shadow, half in the light. Time passes in this moment as our eyes gauge each other. Those pressingly intelligent eyes of hers speak volumes to me as she stands there, not moving. Calmness is still heavy on my shoulders as I take in her image. Her beautiful face, clear and slightly marked by a mess of dark curls on her forehead. Despite her probing expression, I sense a powerful vulnerability in her body language as she stands there, statuesque, thinking. She turns to the door and closes it, her motion shifting the fabric of the robe, skirting it up past her calves. It drops off, showing a tan, unblemished body filled with curves. Now I feel the violent rush of blood to all parts of my body. I step towards her as she comes back into the moonlight, her pubic hair and breasts casting light shadows on her skin. Her body is quite warm, and her lips tingle as they touch mine. I feel her arms on my back, sliding up and down, searching and touching everywhere; my thighs, the little area under my balls and the small of my back. My eyes are closed and I visually trace her body with my hands, surprised by how firm her arms and thighs are. The mountain chill is drifting away and she eases me back on the bed, slowly and delicately kissing my neck and nipples. I sigh in a quiet breath feeling her mouth everywhere in all the right places, then back on mine again. She is moist and her breasts press against me, sliding up and down, her body strong. Another sigh escapes me as I enter her, feeling her on my manhood like a warm glove. For a moment I open my eyes again, seeing the moonlight on both our bodies, her legs against mine, when she eases up, throwing her hair back, sighing and scratching my stomach. I feel like I'm falling off the bed and into something else as her lips keep touching my body. The ground goes away and I'm falling down a chasm, faster and faster. Fear fills me as I fall but the pleasure keeps me close to Berlin as she grinds me harder and faster, speeding up and slowing down. I feel her body tense and she clutches me, her stomach twitching with the stirrings of an orgasm. She bites my neck gently and whispers she is coming, then licks my nipple again blowing softly against my skin with controlled breaths. I can see the bottom of the chasm now, rushing towards me at incredible speed. My body impacts with the floor, and I feel the shockwave course through my body as I blast into an orgasm, so powerful I clench my teeth and grip Berlin tight to me as she keeps grinding, coming and biting me. The erection I have doesn't subside and the ride keeps going, us in the moonlight, falling into the chasm over and over and the second time I come, I feel myself drift outwards into Berlin, then back into my own body with everything fading to black.

In the morning there is light rainfall and we don our pre-packed raincoats, looking like little radiation workers in the green atmosphere. Berlin wasn't there beside me when I woke up this morning, and when I join the group at the breakfast table, she smiles at me and pinches my thigh, gesturing for me to sit beside her. The meal is hot and tasty, but all I can think of while I sit there talking to everyone in the group, is her body against mine, in the darkness of the night before.

Walking outside now, the area still possesses the light blanket of the night cool, though the sun is fighting to show itself through a heavily overcast sky. There is still some distance left for our excursion, as we need to walk up through Abbey Green, past Jacob's ladder towards the Portland Gap and then up to the peak itself. The rest of the walk isn't easy, and more than once I slip on something and fall, feeling my ribs explode in pain as something tough bruises them. But eventually we reach the peak, shortly before the sun comes up and spreads over everything. I am mesmerized by the image, as the sun quickly wipes away the last patches of shadow hanging over everything leaving nothing but the amazing vista. Berlin holds my hand as I take this in, and for a while, I dream of never leaving this position, wishing she and I were statues in this beautiful moment, frozen and ever aware, enraptured and indifferent, timeless like the trees around us, locked into a cycle of existence and death that humans never think about. I squeeze her hand a little firmer as our little raincoats rub against each other in a low crunching noise, the impression of her head on my shoulder.

Chapter Twelve

Conversation has changed. Feeling has changed. As my car drives down Spanish town road and past the outskirts of Kingston, I am doing nothing but laughing. Berlin tells me story after story as the roads become steeper inclines and all we can see is the thick atmosphere of the countryside. We eat jerk chicken at a stand where a particularly amorous Rastafarian plays her a song on his guitar. The next place we head to is a fruit stand overlooking a river, and Berlin is determined to go down there, despite me telling her that we'll have ample rivers and sea to explore in Portland. But she goes anyway, assisted by two sinewy, shirtless young men who take her past the stall and beyond the underpass, where she looks at the river water and throws stones, as the man who runs the stall keeps asking me for extra money even though I've bought fifteen hundred dollars worth of fruit I probably won't eat. Then we are on the road again, the cool air outside killing the need for any air conditioning, the radio playing classic reggae and Berlin asleep briefly beside me, her chair pulled back and the vibrations of the car making her thighs move involuntarily. My mind wants to do the impossible task of both driving and cradling her at the same time, so peaceful is her face. Sometime later, she wakes up when we have an hour or so left to drive and laughingly tells me she did not dream of electric sheep.

We barely enter the hotel room, a spacious one-bedroom tucked into a crescent shaped bay looking out at the sea, before she is on me. Our lovemaking is wild and frantic, loud and insistent. Afterwards, we drive away from the more luxurious confines of the villa and out into the town where some kind of party is happening. Hand in hand we drift through the crowd after parking the car, dancing and laughing in a crowd of hundreds, the bodies bobbing up and down. Near the revelry, we eat dinner and drink beers and head back to the car where she reaches into my pants as I am driving, surprising me by the immediate, rock-solid insistence my body feels and then we are back at the Villa, naked and on the floor, writhing in ecstasy. This continues in the morning before breakfast, our sexual pilgrimage into each other, her eyes on mine, my mind now used to the look of her face when it is masked with exquisite pleasure and just a touch of pain. I know how her hands, warm and powerful, feel against me when she starts her motions, and I understand when her thighs move of their own accord, riding and roaring as she gets lost in the moment. Her breaths speak to me with their own whisper, our bodies speaking over and over. The first two days are mostly like this, us eating and sleeping with each other, love spent, sweaty and relaxed in bliss. On the third day, we walk together on a private, beach, me wearing simple black trunks and Berlin in a dark purple bikini. We haven't spoken for some time today, existing in a mutual, comfortable silence.

"This is so great," she says to me, rubbing my back before spreading out a large towel and sitting on it.

"It is nice," I reply, looking at the sea's perfection smile at me.

I smile at her, and notice her expression is somewhat different, her face tinted with a hint of uncertainty.

"I have something to ask you, I hope you don't mind," Berlin says.

"Go ahead," I say.

"That night we met at the party, when I ran into Kwame Anthony, you looked so disturbed, can you please tell me why?"

I sigh slightly and pick up a stone near a piece of petrified wood and toss it into the sea, barely noticing its impact on the steadily moving waves.

"There is something different about you that I was feeling that night," I say, not turning around. "But it is only because in Kingston, when it comes to stimulating or interesting women, certain things are always in your face."

"In your face? What do you mean?"

I turn to her, and pick up a long, thin piece of petrified wood beside the larger log. With my right hand, I draw four equally sized circles in the sand.

"Okay look at this. Let's say each of these circles represents a different kind of man in Kingston. Say one circle is famous and wealthy people, let's say another circle is ex-boyfriends, the third circle are the single guys chasing these women and the fourth circle is a question mark, meaning a person that may or may not be there."

Berlin nods, looking at the diagram in the sand. I draw a larger circle that intersects all four smaller circles.

"Let's say this large circle represents the women of Kingston. These don't even need to be women who are above average. This circle represents women in Kingston who are attractive enough to the men that want them."

"So everything is interconnected? Because it is a small town?" Berlin asks.

"More than that," I reply. "If a girl is beautiful like you, at some point you will interact or sleep with someone in this circle."

I point with the stick to the circle for famous people.

"Or," I continue, "You will be in the constant presence of these people." I point at the circle representing ex-boyfriends.

"But at the same time because of the nature of the city, you will be constantly chased by single men."

Berlin chuckles.

"This sounds like a normal city to me," she replies.

"Back home in Germany, how often do you run into an ex-boyfriend."

"Rarely."

"Imagine if you saw an ex-boyfriend of yours almost everywhere you went, week after week."

"I guess I would try to go to other places where he wouldn't go," she replies.

"Yes, but imagine if there is nowhere else to go because the options of going out are limited. What then?"

"Then if I see him out I would just ignore him."

I pause for a moment, looking at Berlin's face processing what I'm telling her.

"Let's increase this number by a factor of five," I say.

"So I have five ex-boyfriends I'm seeing all the time?"

"Yes."

"That would be very strange, I guess I wouldn't go out much if I had to see them all the time."

"Exactly."

I walk to the beach, feeling the chilly water on my feet cause gooseflesh to rise on my calves.

"You see Berlin, in Kingston if you go out a lot, every social failure in your life will be in front of you at all times. The girl who cheated on you will be at every party you are, the girl you loved who didn't love you will be with her new boyfriend everywhere you are. The girl you like that you don't know very well will be the girl another guy told you he fucked the same night he met her, a girl he never called again. I will be the guy she calls the next day. The pretty women are almost always drawn in by famous people or wealthy people first, so any girl who looks a certain way will be with a certain kind of person. This means that if you know the people I do, you'll know who all the "pretty women" are sleeping with and after a while, the story gets boring. It's either a musician, well-connected individual or a big businessman who they slept with, men with so much power that all they do is rotate between a stable of these women. Most people don't care about this scene because it is their entire life. In fact this never bothered me until I left Jamaica and came back. I was unaware of how small everything was until I started seeing everything at once. Seeing my ex-girlfriend with new guy after new guy, seeing all the women with all the stories over and over.

I've gotten used to it, mind you. But in a cold dark way. Everything around me feels limited and predictable. There is always another guy chasing a woman I like, always another reason she can walk away, cheat or simply disappear. So I expect less and I feel less. Most of the time, this works. But then I will meet someone like you, and that will change. But then I remember how beauty works in Jamaica, how things *really* are, and I can't trust my feelings. A part of me doesn't want to get involved with you, a part of me doesn't want to trust feeling something for you, only to have you disappear on some guy's boat or get lost in the sea of things to do in Kingston. This is the true caveat; Jamaica is amazing and alluring in many ways. It is overwhelming, the effect it can have on not only women, but anyone who travels here. The warmth, the beautiful people, the dynamics of celebrity and how we socialize, these things stand beside the framework of how everything is in itself a drug, a drug more than I can ever be. So when I saw you with Kwame Anthony, my mind was accepting what would probably happen, that you'd be one of his groupies and that I wouldn't really matter comparatively. But ultimately I wouldn't be losing to Kwame Anthony, I'd be losing to Jamaica and all the things it can give to someone like you, someone here for the first time."

Berlin sits on the sand near the diagram, her tan thighs a vision.

"So you thought I slept with him?"

"Maybe, maybe not."

"Is this how you think about all the girls you meet here?" Berlin asks, trailing her hand in the sand beside her feet.

"This brings me to the last part of the diagram," I say, pointing at the circle with a question mark in the middle.

"Yes, I was going to ask you what that means," Berlin says.

"These are the people that are sleeping with each other with no desire for a relationship."

"Those people must exist in any society," Berlin says to me, standing up to brush the sand from her thighs. As she leans over the swell of her breasts pressing against her bikini top fills my vision, my eyes halting on the dark V the sun has made on her chest.

"This is true, but say I meet five girls in a week, and these five girls are sleeping with "somebody" some nameless guy, how can I truly impress them?"

"Ah, so you have to over impress them."

"Exactly."

"So if you are a guy with a nice car or if you are famous, then you can pull away the girl's attention."

"Yes, or if you are willing to invest a lot of money in taking her on dates knowing that she might be sleeping with someone else."

Berlin lets out a soft laugh. "Oh! Now I see why so many of these guys were offering me dinner and trips."

"Imagine if that was your general experience. Let's say for you to believe a guy liked you, he'd need to take you to a hotel in the country, buy a few expensive dinners and pay for everything."

"I'm from Germany, we don't operate exactly like that," she says, playfully wagging a finger at me.

"I know all about the gender equality scenario on that side of the world Berlin, but imagine if how you perceive a guy likes you is based on these parameters. What happens then?"

"I guess, if you don't do certain things a girl won't like you right away."

"Unless," I say, pointing at the circles.

"Unless you have something that attracts them so much, like celebrity or fame. Indie this sounds very depressing, I couldn't imagine thinking this way all the time. But not *every* girl is that attractive and there can't be that many celebrities."

"The diagram is not perfect," I say with a laugh. "I'm just illustrating the basic structure. A guy doesn't have to be famous, he can just have a good job, or work in an Embassy perhaps, or be a government minister or something. I'm just saying men here leverage power in an unusual way to get women and a lot of women expect this."

"Even if these women might be sleeping with someone else periodically?"

"Yes," I reply.

Berlin walks over to me and slips her arms around my waist, resting her cheek on my chest.

"So how can you know they are with someone else?"

"After a while a guy knows," I reply.

"Yes but tell me how can you really know?" Berlin asks me.

Looking down on her, I hold her face in my palms and look into her eyes.

"I know in the same way I know that you are with someone else."

She twitches slightly as I say this, holding eye contact with her, arms around my waist, the sea swishing in chorus behind us. Her eyes acknowledge my statement by shifting, the pupils slightly more dilated, her blinking now at an increased speed.

"If you know this, why are you here with me?"

I gently remove her arms from my waist, holding her left arm. Guiding her towards the water, I walk in, feeling the sting of the icy water on my thighs.

"Oh! It's cold," Berlin says.

I make no reply as we wade in until the water reaches up to our chests.

"There is a story I heard once, about a man who had a deathly fear of water. Thinking about large bodies of water made him ill, and he couldn't handle going into anything resembling a pool. His fear came from an incident when he was a child when he nearly drowned. It was everywhere with him this fear, and as time passed he began to feel weak. Why was he so afraid of water? Why did he feel like crying and choking when he saw a pool or when he went to the sea? So he asked a friend to take him to a pool one Saturday. The friend went to use the bathroom near the pool and soon afterward the man jumped into the water. He couldn't swim, so he was screaming and thrashing in the pool, gulping in water. The friend didn't hear any of what was happening because he was in the bathroom some distance away. The man fought to stay above the water and luckily was able to hold on to one of the guide rails at the deep end of the pool and not drown. He held on to it for a while, staying in the water, regaining his breath. When the friend came back, the friend was very angry.

Are you crazy? The friend asked the man. The man replied 'no'. After he came out of the pool and sat on the ground beside his friend, the friend turned to him. 'I cannot swim either! You could have drowned!' the man said to his friend. 'I know,' the man replied. 'Then why did you do it?' The friend asked. At this point the man pulled himself out of the water and sat on the side of the pool. 'I wanted to get rid of this fear inside me, I wanted to show myself that I could change how I feel with one action,' his friend said.

'But you could have died! Did you think I would see you and jump in and save you?' the friend retorted. To this the man laughed and said: 'I didn't know if you could swim or not, but that was part of the risk. Sometimes to save yourself from something you have to be prepared to do it alone possibly even die. Only then can the mind believe you are ready for true change,' the man said."

Berlin ducks her head under the water briefly, bringing it back up, her long dark hair slick against her face.

"I love the way you tell stories," she says.

More of the warm feeling she gives touches me again, but my face remains calm.

"Do you understand the meaning?" I ask.

"Yes, I think so, but I am afraid I will not explain it as well as you can."

She comes closer to me again, holding me around the waist.

"Warm me up please," she says.

My lips are near her left ear, and I lick away a salty strand of hair from my mouth.

"Like the man in the story, I know that with you there might be no one to save me if things go bad or if you disappear, but I'm here because I'm like the man in the story, I don't like living in fear and paranoia, I don't like to think all girls are bad, worthless and shifty."

I feel her shudder slightly against me.

"Then why are you here with me Indie? Why are you here?"

I'm kissing her neck and stroking her back beneath the water.

"Because you are here with me. You wouldn't be if you didn't want to."

* * * *

The last day is somewhat strange. We make love in the morning and the evening, but Berlin's body language is different. The insistency is gone, that playful rush to see me naked and touch me everywhere. Both times afterwards I tell her several times that it doesn't matter to me that there is another guy, what matters is if she is at least happy with me in this moment, but she has no response. Her face clouds with confusion a few times and she leaves the room, taking a long walk on the beach. Time passes and we are packing our things and going back into the car, to start the drive back to Kingston. For most of the drive back, we listen to the radio, as the day turns into night and the cool sensation of the countryside gets slightly warmer as we near Kingston. Absently, I start speaking about St. Elizabeth, which has an interesting connection to Germany because of people who immigrated there are few decades before, but Berlin stops me.

"You are so smart eh? Indie? Do you think you know everything?"

"No I don't, I was just trying to having some conversa—"

"Well I'm going to tell you something you don't know okay? Yes, I am with somebody in Germany and he is an asshole. We've been together for a while and all he does is cheat on me with stupid girls. But I know what you are thinking. Why is she still with him? Why doesn't she just walk away? Well I asked myself the same question for a long time. I would sometimes see him look at his phone and smile and then say 'it's nothing' to me, or he would come home very late and smell like some terrible women's perfume. It would make me feel so angry that I wasn't good enough and I would keep trying to prove to him that I was the best. I ran track in high school and I have a very competitive mind. For some reason I wanted to be the best girl. I wanted be his best lover, dress the best for him and let him know what he had, but he would still come home late to our apartment, or sometimes not even for an entire day. But then one day I saw this older German couple at a Café. They were sitting and talking, when they began arguing about something. It wasn't anything important. I think the man was upset that the wife paid some bill late. But the man got up and walked away, and I saw the older woman watching him. Her eyes frightened me, because her eyes looked like mine when I am angry at my boyfriend when I want anything in the world to just make him come back to me, hug me and kiss me and tell me it's all right. But in that moment, I knew I couldn't stay with him forever. I couldn't be that older woman wishing that the man I love had the same kind of feelings for me. So I decided to come to Jamaica. In fact I was deciding between Jamaica, New York and Curacao."

"Curacao?"

"That's another story," Berlin says, chuckling slightly before her face becomes serious again. "So I left Germany angry and a little confused but once the plane left the airport I felt so clear and calm. I was far away from everything and everyone. I had no plans to do anything crazy, I just wanted to be somewhere warm and different. I had no idea I would meet someone like you."

"Someone like me?"

"Stop doing that! Stop acting as if you don't have anything going for you. I cannot imagine how it feels for you to have lost your parents, I am so sorry about that, but you need to stop being so blank."

I ease back into my seat slightly as I slow down the car as we reach Half-Way-Tree, where Berlin wants me to drop her off, where a taxi will pick her up and drop her to wherever she is staying.

"Indie the first time I saw you, I felt something. It was very weird for me because like I said I had my boyfriend and even though I was angry I still think I love him. But when I saw you the first time, something immediately affected me and I got worried."

"The night of the party?"

"No, I saw you before that at Weddy Wednesdays," Berlin replies.

"Oh? You were there?"

"We didn't know each other, how would you recognize me?" she says with a laugh.

"True."

"But Indie, I didn't trust whatever I felt inside me. In fact, I thought to myself he is very tall and handsome, maybe he has a lot of women. I could also see that you came alone and that you were staring at no one, as if something heavy was on your mind. Even though I didn't know you, I felt like I wanted to hug you in that moment, to ask you what was happening. It was very bizarre. But then at the same party I met Marga who is very connected and took me to the *Inside* party. When I saw you talking to that girl in the kitchen, I could see there was something else inside you. Something a little broken, but also something interesting. That girl, I could tell you didn't like her, but you didn't scream or curse at her. What you said about the antithesis of an antecedent was actually cute to me. That is when I decided to say hello, even though my heart was pounding and I was afraid. Something about that moment sparked something inside me that made me feel like I wanted to try something different. But everything is happening so fast and I'm feeling so much. That night on the mountain with you, I've never done something like that before. Things... things feel very real and sharp with you, and I feel a bit confused. I'm sorry I didn't tell you about my boyfriend before but I can see saying that to you would really affect you."

"So you still can't tell me your real name," I say.

"I wanted to come to Jamaica and be anonymous. I thought I'd be here for three weeks, sitting in the sun, getting drunk with new people and then leave and make my decision on what I want to do with my life in Germany. I didn't think about... *this*."

No reply comes from me as I sit in the seat, watching the loud lights of the giant Halfway-Tree LCD screens show commercial after commercial. I take in the orange glow of the street lamps casting the hue over everything; sidewalks, pedestrian crossings and people's arms. In the rear view mirror, I see a taxi pull up behind the car. I recognize the driver, Wynton, who picked her up at the Café some time before. Berlin opens the car door.

"I've fallen for you," I say. "Yet I don't know your real name, or even where you are staying."

She pauses and looks at me. "Everything will become clear soon."

Then, she is gone.

****

Berlin hasn't contacted me in three days and I don't think I'll hear from her again. With a powerful sense of certainty, I also realize I don't know when she is leaving Jamaica. She might already be on a plane back to Berlin, away from men only too happy to go down on her and take her on trips to Portland.

My phone rings, its Brittany.

"Brittany," I say.

"Hey, are you going to Twilight?"

"Twilight… is it that beach party?"

"You don't know Twilight?"

"Brittany, I don't know every party there is in existence."

"Yeah, but you just, I dunno seem like a guy who is in the know."

"In the know?"

"You know what I mean. I see you in all the party pictures online."

"I don't have any social media accounts."

"But you are in all those party pics, smiling with girls and what not."

"I guess."

"So are you going to Twilight?"

"Very doubtful."

"What's wrong, you sound off."

"Nothing is wrong I'm still hungover."

"From what? It's Tuesday evening."

"Uptown Mondays."

"Is that some Ghetto party?"

"Jesus Brittany, the party is on Constant Spring road."

"I don't go to those parties. "

"Let me guess you don't listen to dancehall music either?"

"Not really. I prefer international music."

"Pray tell, what is 'international music'?"

"You know, like house, dance or whatever."

"What kind of house do you like?"

"What do you mean what kind of house, I just like house."

"Do you like EDM?"

"What's that?"

"Egad. Okay, do you like progressive house, minimalist house, jungle, techno, trip-hop or dance?"

"I dunno… I just like house."

I laugh.

"You know who Beenie Man is, yes?"

"Of course, who doesn't know him, it doesn't mean I know his music."

"Do you know Danny Avila?"

"Who?"

"Avicci or Afrojack? Tell me you at least know the guys from Far East Movement."

"I don't know those guys."

"Deadmaus ring a bell?"

"I like Justin Bieber."

"This conversation is dying a painful death."

"Whatever, I was going to ask you for a ride if you were going to Twilight but its okay."

Click.

I take a half-finished blunt from the side table, light it and take a few puffs. Blue smoke curls in front of my face and drifts toward the window. I turn on my Aquos TV, realizing this is the first time I'm watching it. The images are a dream of engineering perfection and form, but I suddenly feel very alone and shut it of. My phone vibrates.

Twilight? It's supposed to be good. ~ Andrew.

I sigh. These parties dipped in identical paint, spread constantly over Kingston's invisible airwaves. Same faces, same people, same girls. Same girls fucking the same guys, guys fucking the same girls, and then girls and guys fucking each other. Idly, I type a message.

Bitches?

I take another puff and the phone buzzes again.

Bitch overload.

I scratch my groin a few times and look out the window. Again, I see the vista of Kingston in the distance, seemingly quiet from my perch atop a hill. Twilight it is.

This is a good party. It is the kind of event I'd really enjoy if I weren't mired in thoughts of other things, drifting between here and elsewhere chasing the question mark. Tonight, I avoid the crowd, staying near one of the bars, slowly consuming alcohol as people rave and go crazy, floating from dance floor to dance floor, dressed in hip clothing, unworried about the future. A few times I hope to see Berlin appear, stepping from behind a tent, or in a group of people, but I never see her face. I don't care about the moment anymore. Kingston feels smaller than it ever has. The music has no effect, nor does the rum on my lips. I can see the dark outlines of hills in the distance and the dark outlines of a familiar future in front of me. I am ready to leave. As the party rages in an increasing crescendo of happy voices and expertly mixed music, I pull out my phone, look at a certain contact and I know where to go.

BERLIN

Chapter Thirteen

Berlin is quiet.

This more than anything is what hits me after I exit the Schönefeld airport. In front of me, is an endless stretch of land. I cannot see a horizon. There are no hills to mark the boundaries, no landmarks I can identify to know where I am. All I see are similar blue skies, but everything else is different. I savour the feeling of unfamiliarity in my brain, as it spins around at settles somewhere under my tongue. The connections are invisible to me. Ideas about where to go, who to see and what the night holds send me a large, resounding question mark. I feel calm with this knowledge. The uncertainty makes my fingertips tremble slightly with an anticipation similar to when I went to college in Pennsylvania, when I didn't know what the town held for me in its bosom.

I'm standing near a bus terminal, glancing at a guidebook I purchased about how to get around. Behind me, I see some of the passengers from my flight, many of them German, walking with the confident strides of people who know what lies on the horizon in front of them. Two girls from my flight, unusually attractive tan girls from Australia, seem disgruntled. Excitement isn't etched into their beautiful faces, and they walk past me quickly on an urgent mission.

"Excuse me," I say to them.

They stop and turn around, nodding at me.

"I'm trying to get to Jannowitzbrücke," I say glancing at my typed sheet of paper.

"I think you can get anywhere around here by taking the train," one of them says in reply, her dark hair fluttering slightly in the nonexistent Berlin breeze.

"Ah cool thanks," I say.

"We are going this way to the station, so you can walk with us if you like," the other girl says without a smile in her voice.

I follow them down a long stretch of pavement, past a few signs indicating where the train station is with telltale graphics. In the distance, I see fields and small houses and lots of greenery. This is funny to me, because I expected dense architecture, tall buildings and people everywhere.

"Is this your first time in Berlin?" I ask the girl with the dark hair.

"Yes," she replies taking a candy from her pocket and crunching it loudly.

"Was the flight okay? Not to be rude but you guys look a little winded."

They both laugh in unison, immediately transforming them into bright, exciting things.

"We've been traveling around Europe for eight weeks," the other girl says, tossing back a lock of auburn hair. "I think I'm just a little tired."

"What's your story? By the way, I'm Caren," the dark haired one replies.

"You can call me Indie," I reply.

"Indie? Interesting name. I'm Anna," the second girl says.

When I shake their hands, I am surprised by the strength that travels through their arms to mine. Both of them, dressed in jeans shorts and plain tops with backpacks strapped tightly to their backs have lean, toned bodies and skin with deep, golden tans.

"I'm from Jamaica," I say to them.

"No way! We almost went there, but decided to do Europe instead."

"Good choice," I say with a laugh.

The train station is some distance from where we exited the airport and for some time we walk in silence, under the five hundred foot stretch of a concrete walkway twenty feet wide that arches slowly forward. I am not used to such abject silence in such a large space. A part of me faintly wonders if a car or house somewhere in the distance will start blasting reggae music, but it never happens. We buy our tickets and sit on the train. Both girls sit across from me and start speaking about finding their hostel, while close to them two tall young men who look like models wearing fitted shorts, tank tops and wire rimmed glasses laugh and point at a magazine they are both reading. An older man in a dark grey jacket with dark patches of red on his face sits back with his eyes closed, a woman who I think is his wife directly beside him, reading a copy of a local paper. There are a few more people in this car, a few with suitcases sitting quietly, some looking at guidebooks like mine. The train is mostly quiet and cool. German instructions come through speakers I can't see and the train moves off. Immediately the feeling of unfamiliarity returns as I look at the interior of the train, with its yellow support bars and grey hand straps, everywhere vibrating with the dull motion of the train as it picks up speed, going from stop to stop. There are no trains in Jamaica and the disconnected feeling of not being in my car blends in with the feeling of futurism that comes with certain first world cities. The stops go by quickly, and soon the calm vista of endless landscapes and quaint houses is replaced by the purposely grown architecture of the city. I say goodbye to the Aussies, when I need to switch train terminals and they give me the nod of people who've spent the last several weeks making and breaking connections with people they will never see again.

With some effort, I figure out where I need to go next, hopping onto another train that takes me deeper into the city, and towards my stop Jannowitzbrücke. In front of me, is another stretch of vast space populated by a variety of different buildings, many covered in graffiti. The deathly quiet from the airport has followed me here. There is something about seeing this much graffiti that is somewhat intimidating. Classical images of American cities with their dangerous inner city neighbourhoods come to mind, places with dark alleys filled with bored young men toting knives and guns, only too happy to shoot and maim someone to make an evening more interesting. But there is something else here. I can feel the last remnants of the city's previously war-ravaged state. Some buildings are ancient and covered with overgrown weeds. For stretches there are huge bushes across the landscape beside clean, well-maintained modern buildings. There is a feeling of afterthought here, a sense that some things were forgotten because they were not important in the grand scheme of things during reconstruction. In the distance behind me, an intimidatingly massive spire rises up into the sky with blinking lights on its tip. As I walk forward there isn't a place I can go where I don't see it. I suddenly feel like a citizen being watched by the all-seeing spire standing silently, unmoving. The state of silence does not change as I keep walking. So far after leaving the station I've barely seen a soul so far, except two old people walking together pushing a cart of groceries. I pass a small supermarket, and follow a pathway under a thick cropping of trees groomed to provide shade for a stretch of forty feet. The silence is suffocating, and I feel if I dug a hole and dove in, covered myself and died, my body would never be found.

I hear no music coming from any apartments around me. I hear no music in any cars. The usual indicators that people live here are invisible to me, save a few people I see sitting in a park, or walking quietly on the road. The first human noise I hear is the rapid chatter of a few teenagers traipsing about by the remains of an old swimming pool. A part of me smiles inside, thinking of the transition from Jamaica to here. In Jamaica, chaos and noise are part of the daily scene, when the men run to your car to sell you bananas or try to wipe your windows, music is playing some *somewhere* no matter where you go, and there isn't much difference between a heated argument and a funny discussion. There, the sense of guidance from the powers that be is different. Here I can feel the quiet undertones of a firm ruling hand.

But, I have probably seen too many war movies. Through the lens of modern media there are so many illusions shaped about societies and people. Some are true, some are only part and parcel of the bigger picture. I stand by the wall of a building covered in so much graffiti the structure seems infected by paint. Following instructions on my paper sheet, I keep walking, until I reach my hostel, a relatively modern brown building, its base skirted with more of that green weed I've already seen on so much of the brick here. The lobby is extremely clean, large and spacious. I am surprised by the breadth of the building. A modern elevator slides lazily upward to the fifth floor, and the lobby stretches forward fifty feet to a table where a young man with a buzz cut types nonchalantly on his phone.

"Checking in," I say to him.

"Name?" he asks with a smile.

"Mark Watson," I reply.

"Watson, Watson…," he says while tapping some keys on the keyboard. "Yes, here you are, private room staying for two weeks."

"That's me."

"I'm Eric," the young man says. "Any questions you have about the hostel or even the area, feel free to ask."

"Thanks."

I pay the balance with my credit card and take my things to my room, which is on the third floor. The room is clean and spacious, with a queen sized bed, IKEA side tables and matching Japanese paper lamps. The smell coming from the room is pleasant, though I can't tell exactly what it is. I drop my bags onto the bed and go into the bathroom, splashing some water on my face.

I go back downstairs, trailing my hand against the wall and back to the front lobby.

"Is there somewhere around here I can get something to eat?"
I ask Eric.

"There are no restaurants very close to here, but there is a
small supermarket maybe five minutes away. Did you see it on
your way here?"

"Yes."

"If you are very hungry, that's the place to be!" he says excitedly.

I smile and head outside, back into the evening. A cool
darkness is starting to fall over everything, and I make sure to
trace my steps carefully as I'm walking. Everything is so wide,
so flat, so ever present. In the supermarket, I browse idly.
Naturally, everything is in German, but the packaging for meat
and vegetables is quite similar. I pick up a few cans of tuna, a
six back of beer and a small loaf of bread. I walk through another aisle, and freeze when I see a shelf filled with cereal
items, most of them emblazoned with the word 'MUESLI'. I
stare at the items for a while, drifting into the past.

On weekends, my mother used to bring Muesli home. I'm
not sure why it was always on the weekend, but it was one of
the few things I looked forward to her doing. It would be in an
airtight transparent plastic bag, the granola bits, dried fruits,
brown flakes begging to be consumed. Soon afterward, I'd eat
a huge bowl of the stuff, whether I was hungry or not. My
mother would make a bowl too, and we'd sit on the patios or
in front of the TV, munching Muesli. She played tennis sometimes on the weekends, so we'd sit there on the couch, her in
her tennis shorts with her feet resting on the dark marble table.
I'd always try to find a comedy of some kind for us to watch,
and sometimes after scanning through a few channels we'd
find some old cartoon I liked or a movie like *Home Alone 2*
halfway through. She'd rub my shoulder as I chewed heavy
spoonfuls of the cereal, while I animatedly pointed at things
happening on screen. She'd laugh and eat her cereal more slowly, telling me she was 'watching her figure' and tell me 'you're
lucky because a man will never have to watch his rear, just his

front'. I didn't understand the full meaning of those state-ments, but I laughed heartily when she said it. Sometimes I'd try and joke with her when she came home after a long day at work, saying 'Mommy! Mommy! I'm watching my front, not my rear!' At that time she'd sometimes give me a weak smile or a dull chuckle, sometimes she'd pat my shoulder firmly and say 'not now', then walk into the kitchen and pour herself a glass of wine. Whenever my comedy didn't work for her, I'd get a little upset, wondering why she would laugh on Saturdays but she wouldn't laugh on a Monday or Tuesday. So, I would wait until the weekend came back around, when she'd be fresh from playing tennis or running some other errand, and we'd share some Muesli and watch TV. I'd always wondered what was so magical about that particular brand of cereal, and now, in Germany it was funny to see that it was so popular.

I cannot remember the last time I've eaten the stuff. Slip-ping two packages into my basket, I picked up some soymilk, paid for the food and headed back to the hostel. In the lobby, Eric was chatting to a fellow named Alan.

"Mark, hello again. Did you get anything for me?" Eric asked with a smile.

"Not this time," I said, smiling. "But can I ask you a question? Is Muesli a popular food brand here?"

"Muesli?" Eric asked. "A brand?"

Eric and Alan start laughing hysterically. I narrowed my eyes at this display, and Eric paused in mid-laugh.

"I am sorry Mark. In German 'muesli' means cereal. It isn't a brand. Any kind of food item that is cereal or used with cereal tends to have 'muesli' written on it. Why do you want to know?"

I pause, momentarily thinking about my mother.

"Just a question, thanks," I reply, walking towards the stairs.

I go into my room and sit on the bed. Walking to the window I look outside at the dark expanse of Berlin before me. My entire life I'd thought Muesli meant something more. It meant love, kinship, something special between my mother and myself. But it was just cereal. Somewhere out there, Berlin was either walking around, talking with friends or sleeping. Here I was unbeknownst to her in the same place.

Was this trip just cereal?

Chapter Fourteen

The flatness of Berlin is complimented by a significantly increased need to walk everywhere. I am experiencing new sensations from the clothes I wear. Jeans rub specific parts of my thighs, and I can feel the pinch on my toes from my timberland boots after I take a thousand steps in the same direction. I'm sipping on a beer I bought from a street vendor while I walk around. The sun is overhead but I feel nary a sunray because the atmosphere still has the chilly remnants of spring lurking behind everything. Despite this, I see a man in baggy red pants walking shirtless with an Alsatian in front of him connected to a leash. The dog barks at me incessantly despite other people in the vicinity. I muse that the dog must not like Jamaicans. I toss the beer bottle into a Garbage can and pause as an arrogant looking man in a grey Range Rover honks indignantly at me, saying something I cannot understand before driving off. My feet hurt slightly and I wish I hadn't worn these boots and I sit on a bench, take off my shoes and look around me. In front of me is the sprawl of Alexanderplatz. I cannot see a road, other than the markings of a train line that an electric tram occasionally drives through. From every angle people are walking, looking like little dots in the distance. There are men on bicycles with heavily tattooed bodies, women in heels strolling nonchalantly into cafés and a few shirtless grungy young men with nothing better to do than play hacky sack on the grass. What holds me is really the sense of space that is so prevalent here, the wide proximity many buildings have to each other, as if they are all afraid of getting close. The area is the size of a stadium with no stadium. For a stretch of roughly half a mile, is nothing but pavement. Two massive buildings are on this concrete tundra, and people look like ants as they walk to and fro. It is like staring at infinity, or God's empty paddling pool.

A girl named Vanessa asks me to take a picture of her with a small Sony Cybershot camera. She is from Britain and reasonably attractive. She asks me if I want to get a beer and I say yes, laughing with slight embarrassment at my exposed feet as I rub them and slip them back into my boots. She tells me that I'm wearing the wrong kind of socks. Boots require thicker socks for less friction. I believe her and she takes me to an H&M that feels forever away and I buy some thick black socks. She doesn't live in Berlin anymore, but she did for a year two years ago. Her trip is random and uninspired, because this time of year is not the time people travel to Berlin to see the sights. It is gray and chilly. This kind of time of year, she tells me, is for people who have lost step in the middle of a search, and need to be somewhere that feels like where they are in their minds, a grey place, one step outside of reality. I agree with her, and as I walk more comfortably in my boots, we go back towards the center of Alexanderplatz and into a McDonald's. I chuckle, knowing her intentions and she goes to the counter and orders two beers. I have heard of being able to buy beer in movie theatres and at McDonald's here, but obviously it was not on the forefront of my mind. I sit with Vanessa and talk about nothing in particular, just bits and pieces about my Jamaican life. She speaks about London and how it is congested and oversaturated with everything and how Berlin was so wide it felt like arms opening to receive her. I told her that the sense of space was the opposite for me. The wide spaces felt oppressive, mysterious and uninviting. I like the sense of knowing what lies in a particular direction. For an Island boy, I say, such a place is initially disconcerting. But I did however, like the fact that everywhere I went, no one knew me. There were no pats on the back, half-baked hellos or people trying to size me up based on my speech and apparel. Today I'm wearing a long sleeved Gucci undershirt with a matching light jacket, black Deisel jeans and my timberland boots. I left the backpack at the hostel, but I have a small Balenciaga tote bag with me. Vanessa seems reasonably stylish in whatever she is wearing, tight black leggings that show the ample curves of her legs, ankle high designer boots and a black Cardigan. She is staying at a hostel somewhere near here, and invites me to join her and some folks she met later on a Pub Crawl. I nod at the invitation, wondering what it would be like to float from bar to bar with complete strangers, getting progressively more drunk as the night became day. She leaves soon afterwards because of some kind of appointment, but gives me her number and I sit in the McDonald's for a while, eventually ordering some fries.

I crunch the fries slowly, noticing a stark difference in the taste and composition from the ones in Jamaica. Resting a particularly large one back into the bag, I wonder if my actions are completely foolhardy. There is no person I can possibly see twice here. Through the window outside, thousands of people buzz around like flies. There are no odds that will allow me to find a girl without a name. There are no odds forgiving enough to create such a scenario. I am not in a serendipitous romantic comedy. I am not John Cusack or Ben Stiller. The universe does not laugh in reply to my jokes and create anecdotes for me to share with friends and family. I am simply a man sitting in an eatery with a bag of oddly tasting fries in his hands, thinking about a girl he may never see. I order another beer, drink it quickly and then go back outside, sitting near a pair of young kids with shaggy hair playing drums. It would be easy to live here, I think to myself. All one would need is a sleeping bag. There are too many places to hide, so many places to disappear.

The spire, though still a strange object to have in my peripheral vision at all times, has helped me to get a sense of direction. When I am near it, I know exactly where to walk to get back to my hostel. The new socks are helping my feet, but I still feel the burn of the rubbing before, and I think of my car in Jamaica, sitting uselessly in my driveway. I drift towards a shop near the base of the spire after much walking, and rent a bike from a shop called Fat Tires. For seventy Euros I can rent the bike for a week and a half. The bike is slightly small for me but workable and the second I move off and feel cool air hit my face, I smile. Streets shoot by quickly and I wonder what is the point of walking to and fro on foot here. I turn into a dedicated bicycle lane on one of the main roads and reach back to my hostel in ten minutes. There would have been much suffering and blistering of toes without my bike, some nameless brand with wide handlebars, a single speed gear and a large black squeeze horn. This change of pace feels welcome, my relative anonymity and my new mode of transport. But I am only here for two weeks. Back in Kingston, predictability awaits me, and so does the mist, lurking in the hills, waiting to consume me. I detour from the hostel and take a quick stop at the supermarket, and purchase a few beers.

I lock the bike to a rail outside and walk into the lobby of the hostel. Eric and two other people are standing there with a young man. A powerful, obvious energy emanates from him. He is of short stature, wearing old jeans cut just below the knee to make shorts, and a large white t-shirt that simply reads "ITALIA". He is very thin, but has wide shoulders, and a strangely attractive face. He has a high forehead, a large nose and bright eyes, dark green eyes that speak volumes to me as I walk into the hostel.

"This is Mark from Jamaica," Eric says to the young man.

The man's face brightens even more as he extends a hand to me, gripping mine firmly even though his is half the size of mine.

"I am Aldo," he says to me in a mild Italian accent.

He turns to Eric and the other two men beside him. "I was about to tell them my story, listen if you like."

Eric, ever smiling, shrugs his shoulders. "I have absolutely nowhere to go," he replies.

"I am here searching for love," Aldo says without hesitation. "But not real love, like I told these guys today, I am on a journey of fucking."

Everyone erupts into laughter, including me.

"Why did you start this trip?" I ask, resting my bag of beer on the couch.

"*Mio Amico,* we cannot discuss things unless we drink, of course," he says, eyes darting to my bag.

I give him a beer and he opens it, takes a heavy drink and rests it on the ground beside him. He folds his hands behind his back and his face drastically falls flat. The bright powerful emotion he exuded before was gone, leaving just a short man with sad eyes.

"Greta was the love of my life," he says, turning his back to us. "There was no one like her. You know we Italians are passionate. We don't like something you will know right away, if we love something it becomes everything. Greta was like that, she was beautiful, sincere and she knew everything about me. We were together for three wonderful years and we were about to get married, but then she disappeared."

Aldo pauses and picks up the beer, turning around to us, his eyes shiny with the stain of tears.

"She was to be my wife, and all I wanted was to be with her. Every part of me, every cell, every muscle, every hair on my body wanted to be with her, but after I didn't see her for two weeks, people started to laugh at me in my neighbourhood. Greta had left me for another man. The shock was so bad that I got sick for three weeks. I couldn't work, I couldn't eat, I couldn't sleep. Then I woke up one day, sold everything I had, quit my job and decided to travel around, having fun, making love to lots of women. I—I know it sounds funny, and I make people laugh by calling it a 'fuck trip', but if I did not leave, if I did not make a decision to do something crazy, I might be dead now in Italy, still in my apartment, wasting away."

The rise and fall of his voice, the pure emotion in his words keeps our small audience rapt.

"The hardest thing was traveling around. Everywhere I went Greta was there. If I met a beautiful young woman and kissed her with my eyes closed, I was kissing Greta's lips. Sometimes I would smell her somewhere, on the road, in a bar. It makes no sense! But I would get the lightest touch of her smell, and I would be reminded of it all; our passionate nights, our heated arguments, the moment she told me she loved me."

Aldo pauses for a few seconds.

"It was the first time I was really in love," he says. "It made me learn one real thing. Love can eat you, love can sting you, but you never know how small the world is until you are in love."

"The world became smaller for you?" came the voice of one of the young men in the group.

"Yes. Thought has no distance my friend. I tried going far away from Greta, but she was too deep in my mind. I could have traveled to New York, to Egypt or to Argentina, but in that time, I would still be in pain. It was not until I told myself that love makes the world small that I told myself the next thing."

"What was that?" one of the young men asks.

"The world is vast and filled with beautiful things and people. If one thing, one person can make me feel so bad, so terrible, then something else can make me feel just as good, or even better. In fact, I started to see that MANY things can make me feel alive, beautiful and fun. Personally I am starting that journey with women and then I will move on to fine wines and painting pictures by the beach."

Everyone laughs.

"But, we are here in the now," he says, his face slowly regaining its former brightness. "Greta is gone, but I am still here. This means as long as I am breathing I can still find love, I can still find reasons to smile, I can still enjoy myself!"

"Salut," Eric says from behind him, raising up a beer I hadn't seen before.

The other two men, doe-eyed young men from Sweden nod enthusiastically. I am immediately envious of Aldo, with his powerful body language and his knowledge of self. All I feel is being tall and dark, drifting in a place where love isn't fun or illuminating. He shakes the other young men's hands and smiles again, a smile to full of purity I feel my stomach tighten.

"We are going to have a drink," Aldo says, "would you like to come?"

I can see Aldo saying this to hundreds of people over the course of his journey. I can also see these people enthusiastically saying yes, drawn in by his warmth and obvious self-actualization.

"No thanks," I say with a weak smile. I give Eric and the other two young men beers and go towards the staircase leading up to my room.

"You can also find yourself," I heard the voice of Aldo say to me as I went out of earshot.

Back in the room, I drink the beers quickly, sputtering slightly at the bitter taste. The details of the room leap out at me, the stark white sheets, the Japanese paper lamp, the matching white door with a silver knob, a light odour of cleaning agents still in the air and the nigh audible trickle of music from some person's room beside mine. My mind does not want to focus on these things around me. I want to be like Aldo, free and filled with smiles and an energy of purity, but I do not have what he has. Maybe I'd know Berlin's name if I was like him, with that groundswell of inner beauty that was so god-damn attractive.

I walk into the bathroom and splash water on my face, watching the drops race down my cheeks, collect on my chin and then fly off my face. I remember more moments like these, with me staring at myself in some mirror, away from the welcoming arms of positive energy in the Kingston's dark belly. I go back downstairs. Aldo and the young men are still in the lobby.

"Hey, I changed my mind, where are you guys going?" I ask.

"Are you sure you don't want to wear shorts?" Aldo asks. "We are going to the beach."

Chapter Fifteen

We roll out into the night with the slick lack of expectation that comes with people our age. The two young men are both thinking of going to engineering school. Both tall, slim and blonde they have the silly energy of immaturity displaced by more a more mature fashion sense. Everyone except me is wearing shorts, the Swedes in a colorful ensemble of blue and burgundy fitted shorts with thin black leather belts and close-fitting tees. I trail beside them, bike in hand.

"Why do you have a bike?" asks Anathon, one of the Swedes.

"Just in case I need to get home quickly," I reply.

"How will you bring the girl back on the bike?" asks Aldo.

"What girl?"

"Trust me, there is always a girl," he says with that groundswell of self-assurance.

A trickle of envy flies over, perches on my shoulder briefly, then goes away. I do not understand this envy, because I do not dislike Aldo. Such a reflected sense of self is relegated for certain humans I gather, people like him and Kwame Anthony. As the thought of Mr. Anthony comes to mind, I am glad I do not think of Amy. Instead I see the face of Berlin, staring at me in the quiet of a mountain cabin, her passion shooting hot sparks. My phone vibrates slightly in my pocket.

We are going to Freidrickstralle. ~ Vanessa

Ten minutes of walking brings us near the base of the spire, where I see a large procession of people. They drift past us, about forty people in various states of inebriation, mostly young Americans and Canadians in khaki shorts and nondescript t-shirts, howling loudly. This is a Pub Crawl. A man waves to me, ready to recruit me into their flock. He walks over to me with a confident gait, dressed in the style of a leader on a relaxed day off; fitted blue jeans and a sharp polo shirt.

"I'm Kenny," he says in a Spanish accent. "For ten Euros you can join us. We'll go to two more bars and then two clubs. We get into the clubs free and you get discounted drinks at each bar we visit."

Absently, I consider this offer, my eyes resting on two girls in the group, faces flush and eyes sparkling with sexual intentions. While I consider Kenny's offer, many of the group hem and haw, asking where Kenny is, unable to continue the procession until he returns. The smile he projects to me is blinding in its brilliance, piercing any regard I have for my own well-being. Behind the group, in the distance a few streets away, I see a similar procession, even more raucous and packed with young people strolling towards another destination. My phone vibrates again.

We are at a place called 'The Beach' ~ Vanessa.

"Thanks but no thanks," I say to Kenny.

Kenny smiles with zero regret and pats me on the arm calmly as if to reassure me that I have made the wrong decision.

"Next time," he says.

Turning to the group he screams a word I don't hear and everyone starts shouting loudly. Two people I didn't see before run around with backpacks containing liquor, pouring it into the mouths of people requesting shots. I cannot imagine where they will end up later. We walk away, the crowd of revelers smaller behind us, disappearing after a left turn past an old building covered in graffiti. I tell Aldo about where Vanessa is.

"Look at that," Aldo says. "A girl you met today is going exactly where we are going."

"Coincidence," I say mostly to myself.

"In a city of this size? I find that hard to believe," Aldo says with a chuckle, turning to me. "Why are you here?"

Behind us the two Swedes chat excitedly about something in either French or German. I tell Aldo the rough version of my story, feeling bored in Jamaica, meeting Berlin and then deciding to come here. Kicking an empty water bottle laying on the sidewalk, Aldo says: "Sometimes a repetitive cycle is toxic. I think we humans are meant to have a wealth of experiences, love, food, travel and so on. You seem pretty well off, why don't you travel more often?"

"How do you know I'm well off?"

"Aren't you from Jamaica? It isn't a very wealthy country."

"Yes but, what makes you feel I am different?"

"Why does it matter? Either you are or you aren't?"

"But I want to kno—"

Aldo stops in his tracks and raises his hand gently. The Swedes stop as well.

"This reaction of yours is unnecessary. There are wealthy people in life, there are average people and there are poor people. You are what you are. I just get a feeling from you of a certain manner of comfort. But when I meet people that cannot say yes or no to certain questions, it means they have not accepted themselves."

We continue walking.

"You are who you are, take comfort in it," Aldo says as we finally hit Friedrickstralle and turn down a winding road filled with the noise of people enjoying the night. "We can spend five to ten minutes talking about what *isn't* or you can make life easier and answer my original question, which is: since you seem well off, why don't you travel more and get away?"

"Who knows," I reply, admiring a woman in a long orange skirt fitting tightly around her waist.

"Many people have an option to leave wherever they are, temporarily or otherwise. Obviously in Europe is it a bit easier to switch things up, but for you to come so far because of possible love and discomfort says a lot is happening with you."

"I think that's obvious."

"Hah! You are still so... how do the Americans say it, 'snarky' with your responses," Aldo replies.

Slightly annoyed by his unending display of positive energy I sigh before making my next statement. "So what is your secret Aldo?"

"There are no secrets only challenges," Aldo replies, turning to the Swedes and pointing at a large structure some distance away. "In every situation I am in, I have one of two choices. I either feel comfortable or uncomfortable. I either give love or give pain. The more I give to people the more I receive."

"Yes, but there are people of all varieties and ethnicities out there. People with different personality types and backgrounds, tastes and dislikes, idiosyncrasies and ways of looking on the world. A person must be in a constant state of differentiation to function in society."

"You speak like an educated man," Aldo replies, pausing by a wall and pulling a pack of cigarettes from his pocket. He lights one, the white smoke curling around his face like a dying ghost.

"What you said is exactly why there are only two choices. Every human being understands love and pain. It doesn't matter if they are a cool, educated Jamaican like you or young and horny like these two guys behind us."

The Swedes laugh.

"You came here with us tonight because you made the same choice."

"I didn't choose 'love' or whatever it is you mean," I reply.

Aldo smiles and takes another puff of his cigarette.

"You chose comfort over discomfort. Company over isolation. Friendship over solitude. Call it whatever you want. Those are just semantics. To me, your decision to come to Berlin is no different that your choice to come out with us tonight."

I nod in agreement.

"But tonight, when the girl is in your arms none of this will matter," Aldo says, stepping on the cigarette and walking quickly forward.

"What girl?" I ask.

He rests a hand on my shoulder and peers into my eyes for a few seconds.

"As I said, there is always a girl."

Standing in front of us is a large building draped in shadow. I cannot place the type of architecture, but it feels gothic, with a large entryway fifty feet high, buttressed by massive cut stones. Sharp spires and towers rise into the sky, their windows dark and empty, devoid of life. Like many buildings I've seen, this one is also covered in graffiti, it's majestic breadth marked with squiggly, psychedelic images. Aldo, Anathon, Chris and myself walk through the passageway and towards an open space. In front of me, several beach chairs sit beside wooden posts that have coconut lamps attached to them. There is sand everywhere, covering the macadamized ground we'd been walking on. Bodies drift in and out of the shadows. The sprawl of sand spreads towards a central area that leads to many passageways. A hundred or so people mill about, and from somewhere electronic music wafts through the night air. Our footsteps crunch loudly only until we get closer to the crowd, where the sound intermingles with laughter and conversation. My eyes sweep backwards and up again, looking at the building, admiring its majesty, uncertain of how a place such as this became a local hangout spot. My mind drifts into the past, wondering if this place was a castle with knights and lords, or was it the eccentric abode of some ancient conquistador. We walk past more people and stop at a concession stand, gleaming brightly with lights that read "BIER UND ESSEN". After attempting to buy drinks, I am waved off by Aldo and the Swedes, who get me a tall dark beer. Nearby people shuffle through the sand, a few shirtless guys throwing it at each other while watch by a girl with a Polaroid camera, some sit without blankets under tents, a few with their own music, inaudible as loudspeakers from a hallway nearby set the tone. Stereotypical images of German bikers in leather jackets covered in trinkets come to mind as I imagine a scenario where I, Aldo and the Swedes get into a scuffle which turns into a bike chase through Berlin. The fantasy leaves me as I see Vanessa in a group nearby, face flush.

She doesn't see me and Aldo is already animatedly chatting to a slim girl with a beautiful face, her gaze into his eyes unbroken as he charms her in the way he charmed me. Two young, very tan women are chatting to the Swedes. Already I know that with their silly body language and model profiles they will probably sleep with those girls tonight. Sand gets into my shoe as I go over to Vanessa, who gets up off a guys lap and gives me a passionate hug. She introduces me to the fellows, one called Big and the other named Chase, men with normal faces and boring clothes with eyes glazed from drinking. She looks nice, in a set of gray leggings and a close-fitting top, but I realize she isn't into me because she keeps asking me which girls I want to talk to. After she asks me this for the fifth time, I go back to the concession stand and buy another beer, not before saying hello to a cute girl sitting on a chair who responds to me by shooting a dirty look. A girl also buying a beer at the stand with me says hello. Her name is Lyska. She introduces me to some of her friends, all platinum blondes with faces bursting with youth and beauty. They are in town on a college school trip of some kind.

Aldo introduces me to the girl he was speaking to who is now magically connected to his arm. He suggests we go to a place nearby, but I'm already walking away, back towards the concession stand grabbing another beer, eyeing a large pretzel. Vanessa is now making out with Chase and her friend Big suggests we go outside to get bigger beers. A short walk past the back entrance and a giant lady in a dark frock sells us Berliners for half the price of a canned beer at The Beach. I'm not thinking about anything in this moment, just watching the large German woman move slowly around as she sells beers and snacks to people, and the animated expression of a young man nearby in lime green pants and a black v-neck shirt dancing for a group of his friends. Big talks to me briefly about hooking up with German girls and how they aren't always very friendly when you meet them, but then he starts saying after you get in the sex is crazy and intense, but I'm not hearing him because I point back to The Beach and walk inside, drifting into a dance floor area packed with giant young men. Looking around I don't see Aldo or the Swedes and I take a piss in a bathroom filled with NameNeko and Hello Kitty stickers. Outside, Lyska greets me with an unusually upbeat smile. I tell her to follow me outside back to the stall with the lady and we both buy Berliners and drink them there, watching people in the distant like shadowy ants in the night. Even though she's never met a Jamaican she asks me why I don't sound Jamaican, and I explain to her that every Jamaican doesn't sound like a ganja-toting Rastafarian and she laughs and gives me a kiss on the cheek. She checks her phone and tells me that her friends are leaving, but takes my phone number, ensuring to send me a text message. My body feels smooth and soft with the caress of alcohol, and nearby a tall, attractive girl walks by eating a slice of pizza. I ask her where she got the slice and she points to a place some distance away.

"It is closed now," she says, "But I'm going to a club with some friends now. You should come."

In moments a fellow pops up, a tiny fellow in a Napoleon Bonaparte style hat named Ben. The girl, whose name is Marie, laughs when I ask her if Ben is her boyfriend.

"Of course not! He is too little," she says in a laugh.

Ben hears what she says and smirks at us both. Another fellow appears, Yohan, also Ben's height. I'm drinking another Berliner, and Yohan gives me a large shot of Vodka from a flask in a small pouch he is carrying. We are speaking loudly and laughing for no reason, and I walk with them off the main road, *Oranienburgerstralle* and go up a dark, quiet street. Marie speaks perfect English, and she tells me it is because she lived in London for a year. We stop at a giant black gate that looks straight from the set of *Bram Stoker's Dracula.* Two men in black jackets speak in hushed tones to Yohan and Benny. They check their IDs and wave us in. I'm looking for my ID, but I realize I left my passport back at the hotel. The bouncer nods at me and waves me in. I follow the group through a very dark parking lot and we enter what looks like an apartment building. After walking up a small flight of stairs, I can hear the heavy bass of house music pounding through the walls.

I ask Marie how much is the entrance fee.

"Its about six Euros," she replies. I nod after she says this, and I turn to the bouncer. "Halo my friend!" I say with a big smile. He is short, but very muscular. "*Mein name ist Indie*, from Jamaica, first time in Berlin!" I say.

"Thomas," the bouncer replies, shaking my hand.

"I am happy to be here!" I say with more energy.

Thomas waves me in.

Inside feels like a dream. Above me is the high, painted arch of what resembles a cathedral, with painted windows and murals running across the surface of the ceiling. The air is hot and wet and looking around I am the only person of my complexion in the vicinity. Temporarily I lose the group after taking a turn on one of the dance floors and end up at a bar, chatting to a man a head taller than me. Adjacent to the bar was another dance floor, and I found myself in the middle of a group of banker types, all wearing dress shirts and designer pants who popped my collar as I did a poor dance routine. Eventually I just lean against a wall, feeling the world throb about me, bass tickling my teeth. The sensations are overwhelming now; the Vodka, beer and physical activity, then a hand holds mine and I see Marie, smiling, her eyes a familiar green from black lights and I kiss her, her body warm and soft, the club thick and wet around us. We go through an exit that puts me on a street I don't know. The purplish-blue of the dawn greets us. I tell her where I'm staying and she nods at me, holding my hand, laughing as I almost fall because I'm so drunk. We head back to The Beach and everyone is gone.

Wobbly, I unlock my bike from the entrance of The Beach and look at Marie. She sits on the bike and motions for me to sit behind her. We make ride ten feet before I fall off solidly, her voice behind me, me laughing as she falls on me and kisses me again.

"We can take a bus," she says to me.

"Yes, let's do that," I reply in a heavy whisper.

We go back up *Oranienburgerstralle* and walk for a few minutes as the sun gets brighter. I certainly don't know where I am and Marie seems confused as well. She laughs.

"I don't know where the station is so well from here," she tells me after squeezing my hand.

Enamored by the rising sun over the distant skyline of Berlin, I almost don't need to go anywhere. Then, a woman in purple spandex pants walks over to us.

"Hey guys, wanna hang out?" she says in a thick accent.

"She is a prostitute," Marie whispers to me quickly.

"We are looking for the bus station," I say to her.

The woman's face registers a bored mixture of displeasure and familiarity with the question. She points to her left.

"Just take a left turn there. You sure you don't want to go into the strip club?"

Marie grabs my hand and pulls me forward, not before the bike falls to the ground with a clatter. Laughing, I lift up the bike and saunter forward as quickly as possible, the lady behind us now, lighting a cigarette, looking around idly. A bus is pulling up to the stop as we arrive, and Marie helps me to put my bike on the front. The streets go by in a whirlwind of color and sound, the journey feels instant. I don't remember going back through the hotel, just Marie in my room, pulling off my pants. She is significantly more sober than I am. My mind races to wonder why there is music in the room then I see Marie on my laptop, doing something, then she is back beside me on the bed, her hand tightly gripping my pulsing erection, her lips on my neck, the smell of the night still on us. Her clothes come off quickly, revealing a gracefully athletic young body. Reggae music plays as she gives me head and I see her transform into Amy, the skin now brown and the breasts bigger, the tongue wilder and faster, the eyes insistent with the need to please me. I feel myself get harder because of this image and then she mounts me, the grip of her vagina perfect and beautiful and she is Berlin now, the body almost the same build, the hands sliding up and down my body as she moans and kisses my nipples. There is no way for me to know how much time passes, but I hear her telling me she is coming and she buckles against me with those athletic legs, her face constantly wavering between being Amy and Berlin, then I come too, shuddering and weak from the demands of the night. Immediately I am unconscious and when I wake up soon afterward my stomach screams. I run to the bathroom and throw up explosively in stream after stream of bile laced with beer and vodka. Then I wash my mouth and fall heavily on the bed, seeing Berlin in front of me through blurry vision, naked and putting on her clothes. As she walks out the door and closes it behind her, I reach out, asking why she's leaving, but I'm too weak to get up and the door shuts with a click, and I fade away saying her name, knowing it isn't real.

Chapter Sixteen

The next afternoon I decide to meet up with Lyska, who has invited me to lunch. My body is still reeling from the night before. Years have passed since I have been drunk enough to throw up. I can barely remember Marie's face.

Lyska looks pleasant and attractive in a peach sweater, a brown jacket and black leggings. I give her a slight hug, my eyes hidden under dark glasses.

"Looks like you had a good night," she says to me.

"Tell me about it," I reply with a slight smile.

I'm pushing my bike as we roam around in no particular direction. We end up on a street called *Weinmeisterstralle* and eat Vietnamese food. She talks about humanity and ideas around monogamy as I listen quietly, eating slowly. Lyska's face is overflowing with youthful promise, a mind that still believes it can change the world. She eats heartily and laughs as me when I accidentally drop an ice cube into my plate. We laugh at somebody wearing a scuba diving suit nearby and I tell myself that in another life I might have liked Lsyka. After eating, we pass by a few museums, none of which she wanted to pay and enter, and go through a small market. I listen to her speak while taking in the architecture around me, still vast and grand in its presence, gaining a slight familiarity in my mind.

She takes my hand as we cross the street, behind a massive building that reminds me of a Spanish castle. We walk past a bridge and she points to a vessel moving towards us in the middle of the Spree. As I stand at the bridge looking out onto the river, fear and anxiety clutch my throat with a giant hand. The boat screams at me, and the water thunders and echoes in my ears, even though it is barely rippling in real time. I see the images of my parent's arms, thrashing and flailing as they fall into the dark abyss of asphyxiation.

"Are you okay?" asks the voice of Lyska.

No response comes from me because I am not there, I am back in Pennsylvania, on the day I'd received the news from a phone call on an old red telephone in the dorm lobby. I hover over myself in this past image, seeing it all again. Two young men are sitting in the lounge nearby, arguing about a video game as David Bowie's "Space Oddity" plays from an old yellow radio the Resident Assistant always had with him. Then I see myself being ushered into the psychiatrist's office for damage control. The sensation returns to me, walking in there with a flat feeling in my stomach, but nothing else. There was no pain or worry, just a sense of uncertainty so great it was incomprehensible in that moment. Three minutes before I had stood in the lobby waiting to see this man, a man whose name eludes me and after entering his office I spend another three minutes getting a sense of his personality from the space. There is something about him in the dark blue walls, a small Rococo art piece on the desk, the noir novel hidden between several books on human psychology on a black shelf on the wall. I know nothing about the man sitting in front of me with the look of concern and pity on his face, but I feel him as much as I can smell the fresh coat of paint the wall recently received and as much as the flat iron office chair pinches my buttocks. He speaks again.

"Do you understand what I've told you?" he asks.

"Yes," I mumble in reply.

The details I'd received are still spotty, but from what I'd heard from my uncle on the phone, my parents had been in some kind of boating accident. The vessel had capsized some- where off the coast of Kingston, and there wasn't much left to report. An extensive search had been conducted but there were no bodies found. All that can be done now is simply plan the funeral. The man is speaking about these details, but I am not hearing him. My mind races to process the things around me. The ticking of the clock's hand on the wall, the rough rub of the carpeted floor on the underside of my Hushpuppies, the mahogany wooden desk shiny with a fresh coat of polish, a bag on the floor, a woman's bag left there, mysteriously beside a set of thick academic books.

"Mr. Watson, during a time like this it is understandable to feel panic, confusion and extreme levels of fear."

"I'm afraid of nothing," I say to the man.

"Mr. Watson—

"I'm NOT AFRAID!"

I scream and run out of the office, my eyes and mind blinded by this new reality. Everything hits me in a wave; the interlaced pattern of the tiles on the ground stretching throughout the hallway of the office, little tears in a patch of white wall not repaired properly, the slight jiggle of a woman's arm as she speaks on her cell phone, the swish of magazine pages as a man flips through an issue of *Home & Garden* in the lobby, noise outside from a Wacker machine, the ringing of the office phone and a woman with a heavy southern accent saying hello, the squeak of some children's toy coming from a room I can't see, and then the voice of the psychiatrist behind me, shouting 'Mr. Watson! Please wait!' but I am already outside, running into the garish sunlight on a day of death, almost being hit by a car as I cross the road without checking what is coming, my heart pounding and my body raging with an anger I don't understand. How can a boat just capsize? How can there be no trace of them left? Everything has a trace, from the remnants of dinosaurs millennia ago, to the stains a faceless man leaves on hotel room sheets after a passionate night with a stranger. There is always evidence. There is always data. Something cannot simply vanish into the ether, I reason. David Copperfield and his minions can make things disappear and walk through walls, but people fall down chasms and are never discovered. There are different types of disappearances. Some are foolhardy some are mysterious but most of the time, there is a trace, a record of a letter that didn't get posted, a missed phone call that wasn't answered, some curious party that was the inception of a question mark, the inception of a search that lead to the knowledge that a person or persons were missing and then the search parties would be sent out, the fear that something amiss would grow amongst friends and family and maybe a resolution would be reached, a statement would be issued by a somber politician, footage on TV would show the weeping eyes of friends and family and mystery programs would probe into the possible causes of certain types of disappearances. But this was not such a scenario. This was a boat, a boat my parents owned that had been going the same route it always went. There was no mystery to their intentions. Most likely for them it had been a boring Sunday and they packed some food and wine and went out to the sea. I can see the image of them sitting on the boat, with nothing really being said between them. Them waving at friends with other boats, drifting along and past some of the Quays, not too far away from any sort of help. There were radios, GPS trackers and a lifeboat. How can they just be gone, the boat turned over with nothing left of them except an idea? No mayday, no cry for help? This more than anything is what bothers me as I run across campus. My parents are now just an idea, a construct of the mind. Something for newspaper articles to write about for a few days and a topic for people at bars to use for speculative conversation. It is the biggest question mark I'd ever experienced. I am a person who questions *everything*. I can't answer this question. I can't sit and work out the details and come to a logical conclusion. Cold acceptance is all I can figure to do, releasing whatever notions I have about their disappearance into the atmosphere as I wake up to the reality of being an orphan.

I stand in the memory, looking at my younger self, running in slow motion across campus, running to an inevitable conclusion.

"Indie? Indie? Are you okay?"

I turn from the bridge and the image of the boat before me and take a few steps back towards the wide sidewalks.

"I—I don't feel like going on the boat," I said in a huff. "Sorry Lyska I don't feel so well, I'll talk to you later."

Lyska looks at me with concern but doesn't follow me as I walk away. The sky is bright again, and I can feel my mind starting to shift gears and move faster. I find my bike and unlock it, pedaling quickly away from the canal. There is something wet on my face, tears. I stop by a supermarket and buy a few beers and pedal for a long time, until I'm by Friedrichshain park and I can't go much further because my chest feels tight and my lips are trembling.

I don't touch the beers for an hour. All I can do is cry, shuddering and weeping with such intensity it startles me. Every part of my body feels tight as the emotions blast to the surface of my consciousness. I did not know there were these many tears in my body. I did not know there was this much emotion. My mind reaches out into the void around me, chasing the question mark as it hovers in the distance out of reach. I cry leaning on a tree twenty feet away from a group of young people having a picnic. They are listening to minimal music and laughing at something together as they huddle around a laptop. I cry on the steps of a building on the outskirts of the park, my head on my knees, the thigh area of my pants dotted with tears. More tears come when I see a family walking together, a tall broad shouldered man with his child perched atop those powerful shoulders, his wife smiling and walking with them nearby. I leave the park when the evening starts to get dark, and I'm wheeling the bike alongside me. The beers are forgotten, as are the people I saw during the day. My stomach growls with the need for food, and the tightness I felt earlier is gone. The sky looks down on me with concerned eyes, and I look back up at it, wondering what version of my parents exist presently. The tension, fear and doubt seems to be gone now, the last vestiges of those emotions wrapped up in my psyche ejaculated through a spell of crying for several hours. I feel mild relief, even though I am alone, walking with nowhere to go.

* * * *

I trail back into the hostel in a cloud.

"You look sad. My shift ends in about two hours. We can go to a place near here and grab a drink," he says, patting me on the shoulder.

Weakly nodding, I walk past a group of young women checking into the hostel. They are dark and attractive in a way that would normally excite me, but I don't smile as they make eye contact, simply staring at the smooth, refined architecture of the hostel walls, the glisten of overhead lights on the tiled steps as I walk up to my room and lie down, falling asleep fully clothed.

A knock at my door lets me know Eric is ready, and we head out in to the early morning. He tells me about life at the hostel, and goes through a few anecdotes about some people fighting, trying to have sex in the lobby and throwing up in the elevator.

"Sounds wild," I reply.

We walk for a few minutes, turning left on one of the main roads, walking for ten minutes.

"We are going here," he says, pointing to a small eatery on the first floor of a building that looks ready to fall apart. "I usually get coffee here before I go home."

We sit down and Eric orders two coffees.

"So what's the deal? You said you were here trying to find a girl?"

"Sort of," I reply. "I was just in Kingston and nothing was happening. Things were getting slow and stagnant. I did a meet a girl from Germany, but I don't' even know her name."

"Why did you come to Berlin? Why not Munich or Stuttgart perhaps?" Eric asks

I tell him about the fake name she gave me, and a summary of our time together in Jamaica.

"This is so strange! It sounds like a movie idea," Eric says to me, sipping his coffee.

"I guess. I think she showed me that I needed more, to get away from whatever was going on in Kingston."

"But what happened today? I saw you with the girl last night, I thought things were going well."

I pause as he asks this, thinking about myself earlier, crying for hours.

"I think, sometimes when you go far away from everything you know, there is nothing left to stop you from seeing who you are."

"Very deep."

I tell him about my parents and the day at the park. The story comes out without any hesitation or blurred details, and I briefly wonder why I am sharing something I never speak about with a complete stranger, but then I understand. This kind of moment is the reason people go to faraway places and sit having coffee in a dilapidated building. Purity doesn't have to be related to how long someone knows you, but just if they have a purpose.

Eric's eyes become serious after I tell him the story.

"That is pretty intense Mark," he replies. "Did you ever cry in Jamaica?"

"No," I reply. "Not once, even at the funeral."

"How do you feel now?"

I take a sip of my coffee, relishing its bitter taste.'

"I feel clear."

"That is good," he says.

"I think so, but I'm leaving in a few days and I doubt I'll ever find who I came to see."

"You don't even have her e-mail address?"

"She left before I could get it."

"No social media account?"

"We don't believe in those things," I say, laughing.

"More and more difficult," Eric says, rubbing his temples. I can see he is tired.

"I have an idea for you," he continues. "Based on what you told me, you are both pretty smart people with bizarre ideas about relationships, no offense meant."

"None taken," I say with a smile.

"You said her nicknamed was Berlin Vanilla?"

"Well, she called herself Berlin most of the time, but I gave her the name Berlin Vanilla soon before she left."

"What's the last thing she told you before she left Jamaica?"

I rub my forehead, thinking about the Twilight party trying to spot clear memories between the haze of liquor-laced memories.

"Something like… 'anyone that is lost can be found'."

"I think she wanted you to search for her."

"Oh?"

"Well not in the typical sense. I don't think she expected you to come to Germany, but I do think she probably thought you'd fight for her. My last girlfriend was such trouble! We did everything together, went to the park, clubs and bars. We had amazing sex, and gave each other gifts, but she still didn't see me as more than a friend. It was strange. Until one day, we were out together and some guy insulted her and I punched him in the face. A few people broke up the fight and I was so angry I couldn't relax for ten minutes afterward. But on that day, she saw that I was willing to fight for her, and then she wanted me even more. She couldn't stop calling me after that."

"So I have to fight someone?"

"No," Eric said with a loud laugh. "I think she left you a clue. The 'fight' is just you trying to take one extra step. You are Jamaican, she is German, probably she didn't trust her feelings with you."

"But they were real," I say, dropping my eyes to the table.

"She is a woman, and women need more than what men need."

Eric pulls out his phone and does something for a few minutes. I take the time to look at the interior of the establishment. Behind the counter is a grizzled, ancient man with large shoulders covered in hair. He leans on the wall, staring forward with a quiet smile on his face, lost in thought. The floors are a dark wood that make no noise as patrons walk on it, and the girls serving us have similar builds, tall and thick in the thighs with long dark ponytails and similar faces. I assume they are sisters. Some people are surfing the internet no laptops, a couple in the far corner hold hands as they speak and a lone fellow sits down with his hot beverage in front of him, the steam rising up as he stares at it.

"Is this her?" Eric says, turning his phone to me.

My lip trembles with shock as I see a picture of Berlin on his phone.

"How did you…," I begin.

"I did a Google search for 'Berlin Vanilla' and I found a blog," Eric says.

"No way, it couldn't be that easy," I say, staring incredulously at the photo.

I cannot stop looking at her eyes, piercing even in the pixelated image before me. I zoom out, seeing a simple blog with only one post which reads:

A MAN HAS A QUESTION. WHAT IS IT?

BERLINVANILLA@GMX.NET

Struck by a gentle familiarity, I feel warm in my chest. I can see that Eric senses this shift.

"A man has a question? What does that mean?" he asks.

"It means that only I know the answer," I reply.

* * * *

It was bizarre seeing her here; the backdrop of the city behind her, the usual ensemble of fashionably chic clothing and Dr. Martens with that buttery skin and those piercing eyes, removed from the confines of hot, sweaty Kingston. She takes me in for some time as well, possibly thinking something similar about me being in her territory, standing on streets she has had claim to since she was a suckling babe. I've never been in such a moment of reassessment, where the call to action has spanned seas. I can see for her it has never happened as well. Her journey like mine, a step into uncertainty, leading back to the starting point.

Possibly what I will always remember about this moment is a large grey garbage can smeared with yellow graffiti between us. It stands there like a centurion, the symbol of our distance and closeness. The road stretches behind her for what seems like forever, and I want to hold her again, save her from the bleak horizon of endless space. We both walk forward at the same time, eyes locked in a synchronous gaze, legs moving in tandem as we gradually become bigger in our mutual fields of vision. Then we are close enough to touch but don't, still assessing the oddity of our predicament, the unlikely reality that we have both created for ourselves. We embrace and we sigh at the same time, then laugh.

"A man has traveled far to see a girl," Berlin says.

"A man has received sound advice on becoming an itinerant sex worker."

After this, we stand apart briefly. It is painful to look at her in the cool light of day, the dark eyes and beautiful face already swimming in my mind.

"I have to leave soon to meet my pimp. So you have t-minus two minutes to throw your offer on the table."

"My offer?" Berlin asks.

"Yes, of social engagement, good times, preferably those involving alcohol and the possible resolution of initial sexual tensions in the glorious release of coitus."

Berlin laughs loud and clear, so hard she leans on the grey garbage can for support, her breaths choked and shallow.

"A man needs to know the name of whomever is giving him an offer," she says.

Pausing, I hold her hand.

"I'd like that," I reply.

"My name is Tanja," she says. "Tanja Mueller."

"I think I prefer Berlin," I say with a laugh.

She slaps me in the chest and put her arm in mine, and we start walking, north of the garbage can, towards the blank horizon.

"I call you, you know, a few days after we came back to Kingston, I guess you had already left."

"A man is impulsive," I say.

"A man is leaving soon," Tanja says to me.

"A man has a three month visa," I reply.

"Good, because the man has something for me and it is dangling between thigh number one and thigh number two."

I laugh again and then we kiss, and again, I'm falling into that chasm, fast and deep, but this time I don't feel any fear, because she is beside me and we are falling together, faster and faster, hands held, towards the understand promise of a future we can't predict.

ABOUT THE AUTHOR

Marcus Bird was born in Jamaica and received his degree in Film Production from Howard University in Washington D.C. He has written for Comedy Central in New York, the Jamaica Observer, several online publications and had two short stories "Gaijin Girl" and "Sleep" published in the 2010 and 2012 editions of Japanese literary journal Yomimono. His first novel, "Sex, Drugs and Jerk Chicken" was published in early 2013. He loves traveling, dabbling in languages and having great conversations.

Questions for the author? E-mail him at: marcusbird@gmail.com
Also, you can follow him on twitter:
www.twitter.com/marcusbird
For updates, his blog and other information, please visit:
www.marcuskbird.com

ALSO BY MARCUS BIRD

Naked As The Day

A young man finds himself in ragingly cosmopolitan Tokyo, haunted by memories of the past, facing an uncertain future. When a typical twenty-something year old English teacher in Japan develops severe physical and psychological aversions to his daily routine in a small town, he decides to move to Tokyo with a few months worth of savings in search of more stimulating horizons. As his physical symptoms remain, and now hit with the demands that come with living in one of the world's most expensive cities, he must take a fast track course in both survival and self-actualization from a host of characters including libidinous transients, self-proclaimed celebrities and kleptomaniac supermodels. Armed with few skills in the face of an uncertain future, Naked As The Day takes us on an occasionally humorous and poignant journey of human choices and ultimately, their consequences.

SEX, DRUGS and JERK CHICKEN

Three completely different young men find themselves in the sex-fueled, emotionally vacant backdrop of nighttime Washington D.C, as they search for meaning in a series of events that force them to deal with loss, love and question it all. Welcome to the social underbelly of Washington D.C, where we see shady parties in dark row houses with illicit sex happening in tiny rooms, statuesque model types snorting lines on marble side tables in million-dollar Georgetown condos and the occasional hookup in a grimy bathroom in one of many seedy bars on the Adams Morgan strip. Three young men—all coincidentally from Jamaica—find themselves together again in DC under different circumstances. Tony Edwards is dash-

ingly handsome night owl who finds that his ability to attract wom-
en—and the subsequent circumstances that follow in a place like
DC—expose him to more than just naked bodies and the occasional
threesome. Winston is a hopeless romantic who finds his life spinning out of control after the re-emergence of an old girlfriend on the
social scene. Bishop, an artist, tries to rationalize the death of someone close to him through a smattering of opiates, girls and his art.
Sex, Drugs and Jerk Chicken takes us headfirst into a view of a version of American culture we don't always see but have probably
heard about; sex with strangers, heiresses who like boy toys, insecuri-
ty eclipsed by alcohol, all through the lens of life in a big city.

www.ingramcontent.com/pod-product-compliance
Lightning Source LLC
Chambersburg PA
CBHW060927180626
46817CB00004B/1423